THE HISTORICAL HOUSE

This series is a unique collaboration between three
award-winning authors, Adèle Geras, Linda Newbery
and Ann Turnbull, all writing about one very special
house and the extraordinary young women who
have lived there throughout history.

THE HISTORICAL HOUSE

ADÈLE GERAS

Lizzie's Wish

Cecily's Portrait

ॐ

LINDA NEWBERY

Polly's March

Andie's Moon

ॐ

ANN TURNBULL

Josie Under Fire

Mary Ann & Miss Mozart

ADÈLE GERAS

Lizzie's Wish

USBORNE

To Debra Armstrong

First published in 2004 by Usborne Publishing Ltd., Usborne House,
83-85 Saffron Hill, London EC1N 8RT, England.
www.usborne.com

Contents

6 Chelsea Walk, 1857

Basement

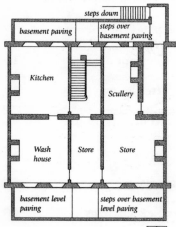

steps down
steps over basement paving
basement paving
Kitchen
Scullery
Wash house
Store
Store
basement level paving
steps over basement level paving

First-floor

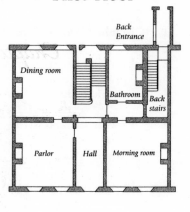

Back Entrance
Dining room
Bathroom
Back stairs
Parlor
Hall
Morning room

Second-floor

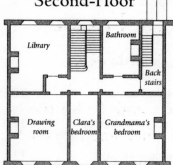

Library
Bathroom
Back stairs
Drawing room
Clara's bedroom
Grandmama's bedroom

Third-floor

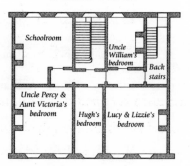

Schoolroom
Uncle William's bedroom
Back stairs
Uncle Percy & Aunt Victoria's bedroom
Hugh's bedroom
Lucy & Lizzie's bedroom

Roof space

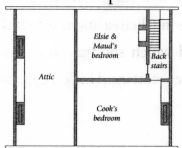

Elsie & Maud's bedroom
Back stairs
Attic
Cook's bedroom

Chapter One

In which Lizzie Frazer prepares for a journey

Lizzie was packing her suitcase, ready for her visit to London. Even though she knew how much she would miss Mama, she was looking forward to the journey; to seeing her cousins again and to living for a time in the fine house in Chelsea about which she had heard so much, and which she was sure was a great deal larger than their cottage. Uncle Percy was the owner of a prosperous fabric shop, and the house, so Mama said, was decorated in the most up-to-date style. Uncle Percy was the richest of the three Frazer brothers, and Lizzie didn't mind that, but it had always struck her as somehow unjust that her beloved father should have been the one brother to die young. Uncle Percy was the eldest, and Uncle William was a soldier who had fought in the recent war in the Crimea, and both of them, in Lizzie's opinion, should therefore have been much more likely to leave this earth before their time than her papa, John Frazer.

He had died when Lizzie was only five, from a fever resulting from a bad chill, but even though seven years had passed since then, she remembered her father well, or thought she did. She could summon up memories of walking with him through the woods near their small house, where he would point at the plants and flowers, and tell her their names. If she shut her eyes, she could see a picture in her mind of herself, scarcely more than a baby, sitting on his broad shoulders and looking down at the world, with her head (that was what it felt like) almost touching the clouds.

More and more often lately, Lizzie needed to remind herself of those happy days. Her mother was now married to Mr. Eli Bright, a curate at the village church. He had moved into their cottage, not having a great deal of wealth of his own. Mama explained to Lizzie that now she was married to Mr. Bright, her money and possessions quite naturally became his. This seemed most unfair to Lizzie, and in her opinion Mama's new husband had turned their home into a chilly sort of place, where laughter was frowned on and every kind of comfort denied. Her mother scarcely ever played the piano as she used to, and the lamps seemed to glow with a far dimmer light than they had in the days when Papa was alive. How it was that her mother, Cecily Frazer, who was so lively, pretty and gentle, could find it in her heart to love someone as gloomy, strict and unfeeling as Eli Bright was beyond Lizzie's understanding, and she dared not ask, for fear of reminding Mama of everything she was missing. She resolved not to think about such matters for the moment, but instead to look forward to her journey to London.

Lizzie had decided to take all three of her dresses with her. One was made of blue wool and had lace trimmings at the cuffs and collar. Another was brown serge; Lizzie thought it sadly plain and only suitable for school. Her Sunday dress was moss-green velvet and rather old. She hoped she would not grow too tall for it before it was quite worn out. She was also taking two white pinafores: the ones that had been mended less often than the others. She had chosen a book or two to accompany her on her travels and her *Mother Goose Rhymes* had a few precious flowers from the garden pressed between the pages.

All her belongings were neatly laid out on the bed in her tiny bedroom, and Mama was helping her to fold everything and put it into the suitcase. Lizzie was enjoying this rare opportunity for private conversation with her mother. Mr. Bright (Lizzie refused to call him Father, and Eli, his Christian name, was too familiar) was always present and ready to overhear whatever they said to one another when they were downstairs. She knew that it was his idea that she should be sent away from home. Her mother was expecting a baby soon after Christmas, and Mr. Bright considered that Lizzie's departure would make life much easier for his wife.

"I wish I might be allowed to stay here in the country with you, Mama," Lizzie said. "I wish I didn't have to leave you alone with Mr. Bright. He doesn't seem very happy about the baby." She didn't say so to Mama, but she had noticed that since her mother had announced her pregnancy, Mr. Bright had taken to reading his Bible in private for hours at a time, and made even less effort to talk with them at mealtimes than he ever had.

"No, dear, you may be sure he is delighted. Eli is

very anxious that I should be spared too much hard work. That is all."

Lizzie wanted to protest that her own presence in the cottage ought not to be called "hard work." Indeed, she was the one (since Annie, the maid, was rather slow and elderly) who helped her mother with the cooking and the laundry and the dusting of the few ornaments that Mr. Bright permitted them to display. It occurred to her also that if Eli Bright was delighted by anything, he had managed to hide it from everyone.

"Your Uncle Percy is kindness itself," Mama continued. "He has always been a good brother-in-law to me, and it's kind of him to offer you a home until after the baby is born. His new house is very grand, I believe, but already quite full. All three children still live at home, as well as your Grandmama Henrietta and Uncle William. To say nothing of Uncle Percy and Aunt Victoria themselves, of course. And the servants. You will be a crowd, there is no doubt of it. He's found room for you, Lizzie, and you must be aware of that kindness and be polite and helpful at all times…"

"I will, Mama. I promise. And I'll write to you, so that you may know about the fine sights which will be all around me in Chelsea."

Lizzie could see that her mother was blinking tears away from her eyes, and indeed, she herself was beginning to feel sad at the thought of leaving, so she changed the subject as quickly as she could.

"I must find room for this, Mama," she said, holding out a tin box which had once contained tea. She had tied string around it, as carefully as she could, so that it would not fly open while she was traveling.

"What have you got in there, child?" Mama asked. "I'm sure Uncle Percy has tea in plenty and you've no need to take such things with you."

"It's not tea," said Lizzie. "It's something else. It's private."

"Will you not tell me your secret? Otherwise, I might do nothing but wonder and wonder, after you've left us."

"It's a walnut in a flowerpot. I took one of the finest-looking nuts, still in its husk, from Mr. Alton's tree when he was harvesting his walnuts and I've planted it in a small flowerpot. I've put the flowerpot into the tea-caddy and it must remain upright during the journey or the earth will fall out. I'll look after it in London, never fear."

"Oh, Lizzie, your papa used to do that...do you remember? Plant a walnut to make a new tree. How can you recall it when you were such a young child?"

Before Lizzie answered, she had to collect herself a little. All of a sudden she was overcome with sadness to think how much she would miss helping Mr. Alton with his trees. He had a large orchard that neighbored their own garden and he was always kind to Lizzie and told her all about the plants and flowers she loved so well.

"It came into my mind when I saw the husks lying on the ground. I wanted to take something with me from home. Something to remind me of the countryside. Mr. Alton gave me the flowerpot. He says I'm to keep it in a cold frame so that it may live through one hard frost before it's ready to sprout. Do you think Uncle Percy has such a thing as a cold frame in his garden?"

"I'm sure I don't know," said Mama. "You'll discover when you get to Chelsea Walk, no doubt. I'll find you a small basket to put your walnut in, so that it may stay upright at all times."

"Thank you, Mama," said Lizzie, and she returned to the folding of her pinafores. She was determined to enjoy all that London had to offer and make Mama proud of her, but it was hard not to feel sad at the thought of leaving home.

Chapter Two

In which Lizzie meets her cousins again

Mama, Lizzie could see, was wiping away her tears with a lace-edged handkerchief as the coach left the Huntsman's Inn on its way to London. It was a very grand coach, Lizzie felt, with a handsomely dressed coachman sitting on the high seat and four fine chestnut horses to draw it through the countryside. Lizzie bit her lip hard because she was quite determined to be brave and grown up, no matter how sad and lost she felt on the journey. Saying goodbye to Mama was very hard, and Lizzie tried to concentrate on keeping her basket safely upright, to stop her from thinking of how much she would miss her mother.

Still, it was true that part of her longed to see London and reacquaint herself with her cousins, whom she had not seen for several years. She would miss her friends in the village school but had no doubt that London schools were full of pleasant girls. Also, she comforted herself with the knowledge that she was not banished from her home forever, but only for a few months. The Frazer family house was near the river, and there would be ships and tall buildings and perhaps they would even pass by Buckingham Palace, which was where Queen Victoria lived with Prince Albert when they were in London.

Lizzie's cousins were named Clara, Lucy and Hugh. Clara was sixteen years old and already a young lady, Mama said. Lucy was only eight, but Hugh was twelve years old, as Lizzie was. He would doubtless be her closest companion. Lizzie sighed. That couldn't be helped of course, but boys, from what she had seen, had too good an opinion of themselves and never allowed that a girl might have a mind of her own.

Uncle William had returned from the Crimean battlefields, Mama told her, "utterly changed." She knew this from letters Uncle Percy had written to her, for Mama, too, had not visited London for many years. As Lizzie had never met Uncle William, perhaps she wouldn't notice the difference, but whenever Mama spoke of him, she sighed and shook her head and said how terrible the war had been, and how we must give devout thanks that William had come back from it with his limbs intact, even if he had lost one eye. Lizzie had been shown where the Crimea was on the globe, and told that our soldiers were helping the Serbs to fight against the Russians, but it had all appeared to be taking place a long way away, on the other side of the world, and Lizzie had had no clear idea why everyone should be at war with everyone else. Perhaps Uncle William would be able to explain it all to her.

Lizzie gazed out of the window as the coach traveled through the countryside for nearly an hour. Gradually, the trees and hedges gave way to paved streets. After another half hour or so, the coach approached central London. Lizzie's six fellow passengers craned their necks to look out of the window, and she did the same. Soon, they were in the heart of the city. There were fine tall buildings everywhere and the wide paved streets were full of people and carriages. The coach drove swiftly past houses and shops and Lizzie thought that no matter how long she stayed here she would never grow used to the noise and the bustle of the hurrying crowds.

Uncle Percy was there to meet her at the coaching inn. She remembered him from the last time she'd visited London, even though that had been six years ago, when she and Mama came to see the Great

Exhibition at the Crystal Palace. He hadn't changed, and was still just as portly and red-faced as ever, but Lizzie was sure her cousins would be greatly changed. Uncle Percy shouted out as she stepped down from the coach, "Lizzie, my dear! It is you, isn't it? To be sure it is. How very grown up you are! Follow me, follow me. Our carriage is waiting and we shall soon be home. The children are eager to make your acquaintance once again."

"Thank you, Uncle Percy," said Lizzie, remembering what her mother had told her and curtseying a little to add to the politeness that she hoped was in her voice. Uncle Percy seized her suitcase in his big hand and Lizzie tucked her basket carefully over her arm, ever careful of the flowerpot she was carrying within it, and followed him to where the carriage was waiting. Lizzie began to feel a little apprehensive at the thought of what awaited her in Chelsea. She felt tired and grubby from the journey and hoped that her cousins wouldn't think her a country bumpkin. She resolved to smile when she was introduced to her cousins and be as friendly as she could to make up for her disheveled appearance.

⚬

The house in Chelsea Walk was even grander than Lizzie had imagined. It was very near the river. As soon as Uncle Percy pointed the water out to her, she longed to go and stand on the Embankment and watch the ships passing on their way down to the sea, or to the docks.

"Very well-connected people live in Chelsea," he told Lizzie. "The late Mr. Turner, the artist, you know, was almost a neighbor of ours for a while. And do you see that church? That is the Old Church, where we worship on Sundays."

The Frazers' house was built of red brick. With the basement, there were five stories altogether, and it seemed very tall indeed to Lizzie. There was a wrought-iron gate which stood about waist-high to Uncle Percy and railings also in wrought iron to separate the front garden from the street. Three wide steps led up to the door. Lizzie wished Mama could have seen such splendor. I miss her already, she thought. How I wish that Mr. Bright might vanish altogether so that I could go home!

She blinked hard to prevent tears from falling, and told herself not to be such a ninny. London was the capital of the country, the hub of the Empire and full of interesting sights and people. It was ungrateful of her to wish herself elsewhere, when Uncle Percy and Aunt Victoria were being so kind.

The whole family was waiting in the front parlor to greet her. Lizzie gazed around the room in astonishment. She felt sure that the whole of Mama's cottage could have fit into it, with some space left over. How fine the furnishings were! The paneling was dark wood and there were curtains of olive-green plush at the window. Several carpets were spread over the polished wooden floors and these had patterns of trees and flowers and fruit woven into them.

It seemed to Lizzie a shame that they had to be trodden by people's feet. If they were mine, she thought, I'd hang them on the wall and gaze at their colors all day long.

"This is your cousin Elizabeth, children," said Uncle Percy. "Clara, you will remember her last visit, and you, too, Hugh, but Lucy, you were only two years old. All you children have changed a great deal in the last six years." He turned to Lizzie and smiled. "I'm sure that you recall your Aunt Victoria and your grandmother, however. They have scarcely changed at all."

Lizzie felt her cheek kissed by her aunt. She was thin, with a kind smile and soft hands, and she was wearing a dress in dark blue wool with a lace collar at the neck. Her grandmother, Mrs. Henrietta Frazer, was a short, stout person, who rather resembled the Queen, and dressed to emphasize the likeness, in a gray bombazine dress trimmed with braid.

"Welcome to London, child," said Mrs. Frazer.

"You may call me Grandmama like the others, I suppose."

"Thank you, Grandmama," said Lizzie.

"How is dear Cecily's health?" Grandmama asked.

"Thank you, she is as well as can be expected," Lizzie answered and wondered what on earth she could think of to say next. Fortunately, Uncle Percy was busy bringing the others forward and Lizzie found herself face to face with a tall, young woman. This must be Cousin Clara, Lizzie thought. She was very pretty, with glossy, dark brown hair and kind, smiling eyes.

"How do you do?" she said. "I'm your Cousin Clara. I don't suppose you have any recollection of the occasion because it was so long ago, but I was the one who looked after you when you visited the Great Exhibition. Do you remember?"

"Oh, yes," said Lizzie. "I thought that the whole exhibition was nothing but a forest of skirts and trousers because that was all I could see, till you lifted me up."

"Yes, I remember," Clara said with a laugh. "You were very heavy for me, and I handed you to Papa after a little while." Her smile made Lizzie feel really at home for the first time.

"This is Lucy," said Uncle Percy, moving her on to where her youngest cousin was sitting in a small armchair. Lucy's pinafore was very white indeed and her shoes were polished to a high shine. She wore a dark red ribbon in her hair, which curled in ringlets onto her shoulders. Lizzie thought that she might have been called pretty if she'd had a more agreeable expression on her face.

"You're very small indeed for someone who is twelve years old," said Lucy. Lizzie would have liked to answer: *And you are quite old enough to have some manners*, but she recalled what she'd promised her mother and looked down at her feet instead.

"Stop being so rude," Lucy's brother told his little sister, stepping forward and shaking Lizzie by the hand. His sandy-colored hair fell almost into his eyes and he pushed it back with one hand. "I'm Hugh. Take no notice of Lucy. She may be the youngest, but she's always giving herself airs."

"Children, children," said Aunt Victoria mildly. "There must be no quarrels or disagreeable talk on Lizzie's first day here. What will she think of us? Hugh, you may show Lizzie around the house in a little while, but Elsie will be here in a moment with the tea."

Just then, the door to the parlor flew open and a tall, dark man with a scowl on his face and a black patch over one eye came into the room. He glanced neither to the right nor left, but strode to the window and remained gazing out at the street. He seemed to disturb the air as he went, and leave a kind of shadow behind him. Hugh, who was standing close to Lizzie, bent to whisper in her ear.

"Poor old Uncle William does get angry very easily. It's as well to keep out of his way when he's in a temper."

"What makes him angry?" Lizzie whispered back.

"It's hard to know exactly," said Hugh. "Anything might. Best to avoid him altogether."

"William, dear," said Aunt Victoria. "This is Cecily's girl, Elizabeth. Lizzie. She's come to stay with us for a while. Won't that be delightful?"

Lizzie trembled at the idea that Uncle William might come over to greet her and shake her hand. How would she bear to look at that dreadful patch? Even the glimpse she'd had of it as Uncle William crossed the room had caused her to shudder. She imagined what was underneath it (a great hole of blackness where his eye had been) and knew that it would give her nightmares for a long time to come. But Uncle William didn't move or turn around. Lizzie thought she heard a grunt coming from his direction, but it was difficult to be sure. Aunt Victoria seemed much relieved when Elsie, the maid, came in carrying the tea tray. Lizzie looked at her uncle's back and shivered. He seemed so angry and unhappy that she felt a sadness come over her as she thought about him. He did not take his tea with the rest of the family but remained at his post by the window, gazing at the twilight until Elsie came in to draw the curtains and take away the tea things.

Lizzie felt suddenly very tired and wondered how long it would be before she was able to go upstairs and unpack. She tried not to think about what Mama might be doing, because she was quite determined not to cry after everyone had been so kind to her.

Chapter Three

In which Lizzie writes
a letter home

October 25th, 1857.

Dearest Mama,

This is a very fine house, Lizzie wrote, *and it will take me some time to grow used to it, when I have known only our little home till yesterday. There is a parlor and a drawing room and a dining room and a library and bedrooms on the upper floors and in the attic, and the kitchen and scullery and washhouse down in the basement and all the public rooms and the bedrooms very finely decorated in the most modern style...*

Lizzie was sitting at the table in the schoolroom with Lucy on her first morning in London. It had once been a nursery, but the Frazer children had grown too old to be looked after by a nanny. Clara had left school and was now learning to be a lady in the company of her mother and grandmother. Hugh went to a boys' school at Westminster and Lucy attended Miss Jenkins' Academy, near Sloane Square. Aunt Victoria had arranged for Lizzie to have lessons there as well, while she was in London. Hugh studied Latin and Science and Geography, and Lizzie wished she might go with him and not Lucy. At Miss Jenkins's, she was sure, all she would learn was French and Recitation and Bible Studies and how to paint in watercolors. Perhaps if she and Hugh became good friends, she thought, he might teach her some of the things he was learning.

Lizzie had always been allowed to look at her father's books at home. Her particular favorites were the leather-bound volumes full of detailed botanical drawings of every flower and plant imaginable, and she also loved *Gulliver's Travels* and *The Pilgrim's Progress*. She remembered the terrible day when Mr. Bright had decided that such studies were not becoming to a young lady and had forbidden her to take out the books and look at them. When she had disobeyed him, he had sold them to a bookseller and told Lizzie that she would be much better occupied with housework. Of all the dreadful things Mr. Bright had done, this was easily the worst. It wasn't just the books, it was the memories of her father, which Lizzie felt had been torn away from her. Her mother had tried to console her, and promised her that when she was older, she would be allowed to read such things again, but Lizzie remained furious and upset for days.

Hugh had shown her around the house on the previous afternoon, and she was still dizzy from thinking about the number of rooms and stairs and landings and attics and from trying to remember her way around them all.

I am sharing a bedroom with Lucy, she wrote. *It is on the third floor. Grandmama's bedroom is on the second floor and Elsie and Cook sleep in the attic. So does Maud, the second housemaid. Uncle William's room is across the landing from ours, and Hugh has the small bedroom next to Uncle Percy and Aunt Victoria's. Lucy and Clara used to share, but now that I'm here, Clara has moved into her own bedroom.*

Lizzie wondered whether she ought to mention that Lucy had not been very welcoming, but decided against it. She had shown Lizzie the drawers into which she was supposed to put her things, and had made it quite clear that her opinion of the clothes Lizzie took out of her suitcase wasn't very high. She had wrinkled her nose a little and said, "Your dresses are not very pretty. Not as pretty as Clara's. Or mine. I guess that's because you come from the country. Perhaps Papa will find you some clothes that you can wear in London."

Lucy had also noticed the tea-caddy as Lizzie took it from the basket and set it on the chest of drawers.

"What's in there?" she asked, rather rudely.

"It's a walnut in a flowerpot. It will grow into a tree one day."

"Hugh likes things like that," Lucy said, making it clear that she didn't care at all about walnuts or about any plant for that matter. "You ought to tell him about it." She turned her attention to other matters, and didn't mention the contents of the tea-caddy again.

Lizzie's first night in London had been the opposite of peaceful, but she decided not to write that to her mother either. It was sure to worry her. Aunt Victoria had come to wish Lucy and herself good night, and tucked Lizzie in quite kindly. She had even kissed her on the top of her head, but it was not the same at all as Mama's warm embrace. The girls had each brought a candle in a candlestick to light them as they undressed, and Aunt Victoria blew these out before she left. Lizzie feared lying awake, because of being in a strange room and feeling a little homesick, but she was so tired that she fell asleep at once. Then, quite suddenly, she found herself wide awake again and staring into the dark. Lucy was snoring gently, like a cat lying by the fire. Lizzie smiled to herself, and thought how mortified her young cousin would be to know that she'd been overheard doing something as coarse as *snoring*.

That was when Lizzie heard the noise. What was it? A shouting from somewhere, but muffled, as though whoever was making the sounds was covering up his mouth. She sat up at once and gazed around her. She could see the jug and basin on top of the chest of drawers, but it was too dark to make out the rose pattern painted on the china. She could just make out the shape of the armoire against the far wall. A line of light was visible under the door. There it was again: a shout and something that sounded like a sob. Someone was crying.

Lizzie jumped out of bed. She opened the bedroom door as quietly as she could, and understood at once that it was Uncle William who was making those terrible noises. She could hear them quite clearly now. His door was open and someone was with him. There was light coming from his room. Lizzie could hear a voice. Aunt Victoria's? No, it was Grandmama.

"Hush, my baby boy," she said. "You're having a bad dream. See, you are here with us in London and all is well. Nothing to distress yourself over. See now, I've brought you a warm drink. Don't cry, dearest. Take comfort from the fact that you are with your family and we all care for you and love you. There, there…"

Lizzie went back to her bed, and sat listening in the dark. Gradually, the sobs subsided and then faded away altogether. She watched the light from the lamp Grandmama must have been carrying disappear as she went rather heavily downstairs to her own bedroom.

Then Lizzie lay back against her pillows. Slowly, two tears crept out of her eyes and she wiped them away with a corner of her sheet. She couldn't tell whether she was crying for her own mother, because she missed her, or for poor Uncle William, who had wept like a small child even though he was once a soldier who had served his country with such courage. I must be just as brave as any soldier, she said to herself. Mama would be worried to think of me lying in a fine London bed and crying, so I will stop this instant. Lizzie made a great effort and managed to stem the tears, but it had taken her very many minutes to fall asleep again.

In the schoolroom, Lizzie turned to her letter again:

I think of you all the time, dear Mama, and long for your letters. Be sure to write every day and tell me everything that is happening in the village. The garden here is very fine, though I miss the red and gold of the leaves on the trees around our cottage. Here, there are many shrubs, and a lawn and a border that will be full of flowers in the summer, but it's not like our garden in the country. Hugh says the gardens at Kew are the best in the whole world. He goes there sometimes and I hope he'll take me one day.

Chapter Four

In which Lizzie struggles to become more ladylike

On Lizzie's second day in London, Lucy pulled her cousin by the hand and took her into the morning room.

"Mama," she said. "Lizzie has not brought any needlework with her."

"Perhaps she has left it in the country," said Aunt Victoria, smiling at Lizzie, but raising her eyebrows as though waiting for an answer. She was reclining on a kind of half-sofa, upholstered in sage-green velvet.

"No, Aunt Victoria," Lizzie said. "I've never done any needlework. Except for a little darning. I know how to do that, but Mama says my darns are more like thick scars than smooth sewing."

She could see from the pinching of her mouth that Aunt Victoria was shocked and felt that Lizzie's mother had neglected her education in this matter.

"Not even a sampler?" she asked.

Lizzie shook her head. "No, Aunt Victoria. Not even that."

Her aunt sighed loudly and said, "Well, then, I must help you to begin one, and see that you learn the stitches. I would have expected you, at your age, to have mastered the first steps of the embroidery skills that should be part of every young lady's education. Lucy is only eight years old but finished her first sampler last year. Come and sit beside me and we'll begin on this piece of canvas. Here is your needle, and

I will ask Elsie to find a sewing basket for you. I am sure there must be one somewhere that you can use."

Lucy smirked and simpered when her mother's attention was on Lizzie. Aunt Victoria didn't notice, but Lizzie saw her and wished she could put out her tongue at her young cousin.

By the time she and Lucy returned to the schoolroom, Lizzie had decided that embroidery was definitely the most tedious occupation in the whole world. She'd sat for an hour or more, dragging a thread of green in a silver needle through the canvas again and again, and all the while she was aware that her cousin and her aunt were sewing away at great speed, making tiny, dainty stitches in the fine linen they were hemming. Aunt Victoria looked over at Lizzie's work and said, "Well, it is your first time, after all. Perhaps it is a mistake to expect too much today. I daresay you will improve with practice."

Lucy was less kind than her mama. Once they were in the schoolroom, she remarked, "Your stitches are too big. My stitches are very small and dainty. Mama said so. She said I am an excellent embroiderer."

"I don't want to be any kind of embroiderer. I hate it. I'd much rather be in the garden with real flowers than making one from threads on a canvas."

"That's because you come from the country, where flowers are more common, I suppose. Here in London, we like our flowers on samplers, in paintings or in vases on the sideboard."

Lizzie wanted to say: *That's very foolish of you. Flowers are best in their natural setting,* but it was almost time for lunch and she didn't want to argue in front of the others, so she remained silent and contented herself with making a face at Lucy's back as she left the room. Lizzie already missed helping Mr. Alton in his orchard and she made up her mind that when she was quite grown up and could do what she pleased, she would find some way to work every day with growing things. She wondered if there were such people in the world as lady gardeners.

All the gardeners she had ever heard of were men.

In the dining room, the whole family sat around an enormous table, covered in a cloth of dazzling white linen. Lizzie was relieved to be seated far away from Uncle William, who stared down at his plate without meeting anyone's gaze. From time to time he took a mouthful of food, but he was deep in his own thoughts. Lizzie wondered why no one tried to speak to him. Perhaps they were as nervous of what he might say as she was. He looked just like a giant in a storybook, hunched over his plate and frowning at the food as though he were displeased by it. She couldn't help fearing that if he were to open his mouth, what would come out would be not words, but terrifying groans and shouts.

Elsie brought in the mutton and vegetables and as soon as she had served everyone, Clara spoke. "I was visiting Papa's shop this morning when Mrs. Barrett came in. She was telling us about Florence Nightingale. She saw her last week, stepping into her carriage. Can you imagine? I should love to make her acquaintance. In fact, I should like to be a nurse myself, and look after the sick and wounded as she did. Mrs. Barrett says that Miss Nightingale has started a school for nurses. I would like more than anything in the world to enroll in that school, Papa. Please, please say that I may approach the hospital – St Thomas's I believe – and make inquiries. Please?"

Uncle Percy was so taken aback by this remark that he blinked and paused with a forkful of potato halfway to his lips.

"When you were younger, I remember," said Aunt Victoria, putting down her fork and frowning at her daughter, "you did indeed bandage your dolls' limbs, and pretend that your dolls' house was the hospital at Scutari, but your Uncle William was fighting in the Crimea then. It was only natural for you to imagine yourself helping him and others like him. But I think nursing is a most unsuitable profession for a well brought-up young lady."

Clara's cheeks were pink as she answered her mother. "I think the work would suit me."

"Fiddlesticks," said Grandmama, her voice echoing a little in the high-ceilinged room. "Childish games are a very different matter from the real care of the sick. Just think of the blood, Clara dear. And the possibility of catching so many dreadful diseases. The thought of a grandchild of mine wiping all manner of disgusting *substances* from the faces and bodies of the sick…well, it turns my stomach, I admit it."

Clara whispered under her breath, "But it is not you, Grandmama, who would be attending to the invalids. It would be me, would it not? I know my own mind."

"There is time enough for you to decide such things when you're older," said Uncle Percy. "You are only sixteen years old. We will consider the matter next year, perhaps."

"But surely it would do no harm to make a few inquiries?" Clara asked. Her cheeks were scarlet now and Lizzie could see that she was making a great effort to keep her temper.

"I have no wish to discuss such things at the moment, Clara," said Aunt Victoria. "We will consider your future again at a later date. For the moment, we must put thoughts of you nursing out of our minds and simply give thanks to Miss Nightingale and her ilk for all their sterling work during the late war."

"She's an angel," said Uncle William, in a voice that sounded to Lizzie as if it were very seldom used. It was harsh and grating as if every word cost Uncle William pain to utter it. "I saw her, you know. At Scutari."

"Indeed you did," said Aunt Victoria, and everyone at the table turned toward Uncle William, eager to see what he said next, but he had fallen silent again, and began to move the food from the plate to his lips once more with a frown on his face.

Clara went on: "I could be an angel like Miss Nightingale. And I wouldn't mind the blood. Nor the vomit. I'm not easily disgusted."

"This is not a fit subject for the lunch table," said Aunt Victoria. "Stop it at once, child. Let us talk about something else."

Lucy was making a horrified face. "Ugh!" she said. "Vomit! Clara, that's disgusting."

"No it's not," said Clara. "It's part of our nature. I'm sure I wouldn't mind that side of it."

"I must return to work," said Uncle Percy. He had finished the food on his plate and put his knife and fork down with a clatter. "I see no reason to continue talking about this matter now, Clara. We will see what the future will bring but for the moment your duty is to learn all the accomplishments that befit a young lady. I'm sure you have a very pleasant life."

"It's pleasant enough, Papa, but not *useful*," said Clara. "I would like to be of some purpose in the world. And I should like to study something more interesting than the latest fashions. Hugh does, and I don't see why I may not."

Lizzie could see that Uncle Percy might have lost

his temper, but chose instead to be amused by Clara's outburst. He laughed and said, "Learning indeed! Whatever next? Whoever heard of such a thing? Besides, Hugh is a boy and a young man must have an education. You will marry in the fullness of time and your duty will be to support and care for your husband. Like your Mama." He smiled at Aunt Victoria.

Hugh, who was sitting opposite Lizzie, said, "I'm going to be a plant collector. I shall study botany and then I'll discover thousands of strange new trees and shrubs and flowers and bring them home to Kew Gardens and they will all be named after me. I won't have time to help Papa in the shop."

Uncle Percy stood up. "Well, this argument will not put bread upon the table. You, Hugh, are very young still and there is time for you to acquire some sense and reason. Your dreams are quite suitable for a child and will change as you grow older, mark my words. And naturally, when I retire, you will take over the business."

He made his way to the door and turned to speak to Clara again, "And you, my dear, are old enough to know your duties to this family."

☙

Now, Lizzie was sitting at the table in the schoolroom, writing her daily letter to her mother. She thought of Clara, made to accompany her own mama as she sat in one drawing room after another and to make polite conversation with other young ladies, and understood that this was as unwelcome to Clara as stitching samplers was to her. She felt sorry for her eldest cousin, whom she admired greatly for her pretty face and kind manner. She was also full of admiration for Clara's ambition. Lizzie sighed as she bent her head over her letter again and went on writing: *Uncle William spoke a little today at lunch. He made a remark about Florence Nightingale. Clara wants to train in Miss Nightingale's new school for nurses, but Aunt Victoria does not approve and will do all she can to prevent it, I fear.*

I would like to do what Hugh says he wants to do, and travel the world looking for strange plants to bring back and grow here in England. That would be wonderful, would it not? I think that if women can study to become nurses, they should also be allowed to study botany. Grandmama said that meals in the family were becoming as argumentative as a sitting of Parliament.

Chapter Five

In which Lizzie and Hugh disagree

After only a few days in London, Lizzie felt as though she were settling into the routines of the house. She still missed her mother. Even though Mama often sent letters, Lizzie wondered how life really was for her, alone with the gloomy Mr. Bright (whose name had always struck her as quite laughably inappropriate). But, for the most part, the time passed pleasantly enough. The lessons at Miss Jenkins's Academy were not difficult, but neither were they as interesting as Lizzie would have wished. Nevertheless, she found her classmates very agreeable. Lizzie and Lucy were accompanied to school by Elsie, the maid, who also met them and walked home with them after their midday meal, which they ate at school.

The daily hour in the morning room (from three o'clock to four o'clock) was the worst time of the day for Lizzie. She couldn't understand why it was named the *morning* room when they generally frequented it after *lunch*. She and Lucy would sit with Aunt Victoria and attend to their handiwork. Lizzie looked often at the clock on the mantelpiece and wished the hands would move a little more quickly. This clock was much plainer than the one in the drawing room, which was covered in gold curlicues and twiddles. Also, in the drawing room, there was an arrangement of wax flowers under a glass dome, and many china figurines of shepherdesses in pretty skirts.

These delicate creatures didn't look to Lizzie as though they'd ever been near a real sheep. She thought of Hugh, doing his sums and writing his compositions upstairs in the schoolroom, and longed to be allowed to learn the same things as he – his lessons were surely more interesting than tedious embroidery. She had glanced at his books sometimes when she had been writing letters, and had been intrigued to see the maps and diagrams and words in foreign languages.

Lizzie's sampler was now a little grubby around the edges, where she had gripped it so hard. Though her stitches were growing more even, they were still considered too large by Aunt Victoria, and she hadn't even finished the row of letters of the alphabet. There had been a good deal of unpicking. After the letters, there would be the numbers to complete and only then could she progress to the picture of a house and a tree. At her present rate of progress, it seemed as though she might never finish. At least when she was in her mother's care again, she would be spared this daily torment.

As soon as she had put away her sewing, Lucy ran out of the room. She was doubtless going down to the basement to talk to Cook and play with the cat, whose name was Mrs. Tibbs. When once Lizzie had suggested that she might accompany Lucy, she was told, rather firmly: "Mrs. Tibbs is my pet, and you can't stroke her unless I give you permission."

Lizzie didn't want to play with Mrs. Tibbs today anyway. She had something else on her mind. When Aunt Victoria indicated that she was allowed to put her needlework away, Lizzie went to find Hugh. She had been so busy getting used to her new life in London that she hadn't had the chance to tend to the walnut she had brought with her from the country. The frost would soon be here, and the flowerpot needed to be outdoors, under some kind of shelter. She had discovered that there was a cold frame in the garden, which would do very well for her purposes.

It looked like an enormous box with glass sides and a glass lid, which could be lifted up when the plants needed attention. A wizened old man named Amos Lewin came to tend the garden twice a week, and Lizzie had seen him, pottering about among the shrubs, often accompanied by Hugh. On one or two occasions, Lizzie had gone out to the garden while he was there, and tried to engage him in conversation, but he was a very quiet sort of man and for the most part she simply followed him around, looking at what he was doing and enjoying the sight of all the plants that he took care of. He was not at work today, but Hugh would help her to find the perfect place for her flowerpot.

Now that she was free of her wretched sampler, Lizzie flew up the stairs two at a time. Lucy was just on the point of going down to the kitchen and her voice reached Lizzie on the first landing.

"Mama would make you come downstairs and walk up again properly. She'd say you were a *hoyden*."

Lucy produced this last word with an air of great satisfaction.

"Then it's fortunate Aunt Victoria is otherwise occupied," said Lizzie, looking down at her cousin from the turn of the stair. Lucy tossed her curls and went down to the basement without another word. Lizzie ran up the next flight of stairs and opened the door of the schoolroom, and there was Hugh, drawing something very complicated in a sketchbook.

"Hugh?" Lizzie stood at his shoulder.

"Hmm?" Hugh was concentrating on his work and put down his pencil reluctantly. "I'm busy, Lizzie." He laughed. "Busy Lizzie. How very amusing…that's the name of a plant, don't you see?"

"I know. Hugh, I need you to help me, please. I have something that needs to go in the cold frame. I don't want Mr. Lewin to be put out by finding something unexpected in a place he's reserved for some other plant."

"What have you got? Where did you get it? You've

hardly been out of the house, apart from going to school."

This was true. Lizzie had been on a few short walks, in the company of Grandmama, along the Embankment. She had visited *Frazer and Son* only a few days ago, together with Aunt Victoria and Clara, to buy a length of blue wool for a new dress that would be made up by Grandmama's own seamstress in time for Christmas. Now she said to Hugh, "I brought it with me from the country. It's a walnut, and I mean to grow it into a tree. I hope you will help me."

"I'm sure your walnut would do better indoors," said Hugo. "The warmth of the house will help it to germinate."

"No," said Lizzie. "Mr. Alton, whose tree this walnut comes from, was most particular. The nut needs a hard frost to help it grow."

"Frost kills a young plant. Everyone knows that."

Lizzie wondered whether Hugh could possibly be right. He did, after all, spend a great deal of time reading about plants and animals, and she knew only what she'd been told. Perhaps Mr. Alton was mistaken. Then she remembered the noble trees in the garden of his property in the village and knew that he wasn't. She said, "It's my walnut and I want to put it out in the cold frame."

"You're being stupid!" said Hugh. "You're just as stubborn as any other girl I've ever met. Girls never listen to reason. They don't know a thing about science."

"That's not true!" Lizzie protested. "I am *not* stubborn. I simply know what's right. I've been told by someone who's been harvesting walnut trees for years."

"When Mr. Lewin comes next week," said Hugh, "we can ask him, but I'm sure he'll agree with me."

"But I wanted my flowerpot to go outside this afternoon. Or tomorrow at the latest. Won't you help me? We can ask Mr. Lewin as well, but meanwhile…"

"You're the one who's going to cry when that nut doesn't sprout," said Hugh.

"Then you *will* help me? Oh, please do! I'm sure it's the right thing, truly."

"I can see that I'll be nagged and nagged if I don't do what you ask. You won't stop asking me, will you?"

"Certainly not. I shall continue till you give in."

Hugh sighed. "Tomorrow after school, then. I promise."

"Thank you. It'll be a wonderful walnut tree one day, you know. They grow slowly but they are very splendid when they're mature."

"Enough! I don't want to hear another word about your silly walnut. You're not only stubborn, like all girls, but also too fond of the sound of your own voice. Like all girls." Now that Hugh had promised to help her, Lizzie didn't mind his teasing so much, but she still picked up a book from the table and held it up in mock anger.

"Take back those rude remarks, Hugh, or I shall throw this book at your head."

Hugh burst out laughing. "I surrender! You're too

fierce for me. I'm going to hide behind the rocking horse."

When Lucy came to call her brother and her cousin for supper, she found them chasing around the room, helpless with laughter.

"Whatever are you two up to?" she asked. "Lizzie looks a fright. Don't you think she looks a fright, Hugh? Mama will make you go upstairs again and brush your hair, Lizzie."

"Then I'd better go and do it before she sees me, hadn't I?" said Lizzie. She left the room, smiling at Hugh from behind Lucy's back.

Chapter Six

In which the family visits Kew Gardens

On the following Sunday, which was the clearest, brightest November day Lizzie had ever seen, the Frazer family, all except for Uncle William, set out for Kew Gardens in the carriage. The horses had been specially brushed and groomed by their stable boys, in the livery stables where they were housed, and the Frazer family, Lizzie thought, looked just as fine.

Everyone was in their Sunday best and Aunt Victoria's hat was decorated with pheasant's feathers. She had brought a gray fur muff with her, for there was a chill in the air. Grandmama had a fox fur around her neck, which Lizzie disliked intensely. The dead fox seemed to look out of his glass eyes so very sadly.

"The trees will be magnificent," said Uncle Percy. "And there will be far fewer people than we might have met during the summer months. I can never understand why everyone so admires the natural world in May, June and July and quite loses interest in October and November."

"It's often very chilly during those months, dear," said Aunt Victoria, "and the flowers are mostly over by the autumn, are they not?"

Lizzie was staring silently out of the window. She looked at the river as they crossed Putney Bridge and could see the dome of St. Paul's Cathedral in the far distance. Her thoughts turned to her walnut, which was now safely installed in the cold frame. Even though he had complained, Hugh had helped her to find the right spot and it made her feel happy to think of it there, safe with the other plants.

She was relieved that she no longer had to worry about her flowerpot, for something else had begun to concern her. Up until now, every day had brought a letter from Lizzie's mama to her daughter. Lizzie longed for each delivery, and used to stand near the window of the front parlor, looking out for the mailman, who waved cheerily to her as he came to the door.

But for the last three days, there had been no word from Mama. At first, Lizzie was disappointed but not worried. It was possible that Mama was busy. Perhaps she and Mr. Bright had gone on a trip to visit a friend, though Lizzie found it hard to imagine who this might be. She determined not to fret, but as the days went by, it was hard not to imagine that something bad might have happened to her mother. The baby she was expecting was not due until the new year, but ladies, she knew, were sometimes unwell in the months before their babies were born.

She was determined not to say anything about it to anyone. Perhaps there would be a letter tomorrow. On this brilliantly sunny day, it was hard not to be optimistic and think that nothing was amiss. She was on her way to Kew Gardens, which Hugh said were the best in the whole world.

The gardens surpassed all Lizzie's expectations. The trees had lost most of their gold and scarlet leaves, but these lay about the ground in heaps, and the children crunched through them, shouting with delight. The wide paths between stretches of lawn were filled, on this fine day, with families enjoying the beauties of nature tamed. Clara and Lucy went off to walk with Uncle Percy around the lake and the others made their way toward an enormous greenhouse.

"This is the best thing in the whole of Kew," said Hugh to Lizzie. "It's just like a real jungle in there. Let's go in."

The greenhouse was the most beautiful building

that Lizzie had ever seen, and reminded her of the Crystal Palace, where the Great Exhibition had been held. It was very high, with a curved roof that glittered in the sun, and all the beams and joints of the building were made of white wrought iron. She could see the dark green leaves of a plant she didn't recognize pressing against the panes. Aunt Victoria and Grandmama found a bench to rest on, and Hugh and Lizzie went inside.

The heat, the steamy air and the mossy, earthy smells in the greenhouse made Lizzie feel faint at first, but she followed Hugh up one of the paths, marveling at the lush greenery all around. At one end, a spiral staircase twisted up and up to the highest panes of all, and there were some trees that were almost tall enough to press against the glass roof. On a long trestle table at the far end of one of the gravel paths, an elderly gentleman was busy with pots and compost.

"Let's ask him," Hugh whispered to Lizzie.

"Ask him what?"

"About your silly walnut, of course. I'm sure it should be indoors."

"But we don't know him. Maybe he doesn't wish to be disturbed," Lizzie whispered back. Hugh wasn't listening. He had already approached the old man and was speaking to him.

"Good morning, sir," he said, and the elderly gentleman turned around.

"Good morning, lad," he said. "May I be of assistance? Mr. Samuel Hocking at your service."

"I'm Hugh Frazer and this is my cousin, Lizzie."

"Charmed, I'm sure," said Mr. Hocking and he bowed from the waist, with his fingers still covered with crumbs of dark brown earth. He looked, Lizzie thought, exactly like an elderly elf, being exceedingly small and red-faced, with a sparse, white beard.

"May I ask you a question, sir?" Hugh asked. "My cousin and I have been having a disagreement about a walnut."

"I'll help you if I can," said Mr. Hocking. "You are

trying to grow a walnut tree from a nut, I take it?"

"Yes, sir," said Lizzie, feeling braver now that Mr. Hocking had turned out to be so friendly. "I brought it to London from the country and I was told that it needed a hard frost to help it grow. Hugh says that warmth is good for plants, and indeed it is very warm in this greenhouse."

"Many of the plants here are tropical," said Mr. Hocking, "but you're definitely right, Miss. A frost is just what's required. Perhaps there's a cold frame in your garden?"

"Yes, that's where we've put it," said Hugh.

"You thought it should remain indoors," Lizzie reminded him. "You didn't believe me, when I told you what Mr. Alton said."

"One should always, I've found, listen to the ladies," said Mr. Hocking.

"Thank you," said Lizzie. She made a face at Hugh. "I am going to plant it in the garden at the back of the house, when it's big enough."

"That will be delightful," said Mr. Hocking. "You should see some shoots coming from your nut early next year. Perhaps in February or March. They're slow to grow, are walnuts. That's what I love about these here…" He waved a hand at the variety of leaves and shoots that surrounded them in the jungle-like atmosphere of the greenhouse. "They grow up like Jack's beanstalk." He chuckled. "Yes, just like magic. Inches and inches almost overnight, it seems sometimes. But when it comes to walnuts, patience is the order of the day. Yes, that's it. Great patience."

The children said goodbye to their new friend and Hugh promised that they would return and see him on another occasion.

"Yes, indeed," said Mr. Hocking. "Now that I know about the walnut, I must be kept informed of its progress."

☙

While the family had been at Kew Gardens, and even on the drive back to Chelsea, Lizzie had managed not to think too much about her mother and what could possibly account for the fact that no letters had been delivered to the house recently. Once they reached home, however, and particularly once everyone had eaten supper and Lizzie was in the schoolroom with Lucy and Hugh, every kind of worrying thought began to come into her mind.

She wondered whether to tell anyone about her fears. Lucy asked her to join in a game of *Beggar my Neighbor*, but Lizzie wasn't in the mood for games. "I'm sorry, Lucy," she said. "I don't feel very much like playing tonight."

"Why?" said Lucy. "Are you ill? I shall tell Mama if you are."

"No, I'm well enough. Perhaps a little tired after our trip to Kew."

Hugh looked up from his chair. He was reading a book about the animals of the African continent, but he put it down at once. "I'm not tired," he said. "Even Lucy isn't tired. I think you're keeping something from us. You look strange, as if you're about to burst into tears. You're not, are you? I can't bear it when girls start sobbing."

"I never cry," said Lucy, complacently. "I haven't cried since I was six."

"Yes, you have," said Hugh. "You cried when Mama sent you to your room for disobeying her, just the other day."

"I was angry, that's all. Angry tears don't count. They're not real tears, are they? Not like sad tears."

"I'm not sad," Lizzie said. "But I *am* a little worried. I don't know if I'm right to be, but I can't help it."

"Can't help what?" said Clara. She had come into the schoolroom to see whether the others were ready to prepare for bed.

"Lizzie's worried," said Lucy. "She won't tell us why."

Clara came and put her arm around Lizzie's shoulders at once.

"Oh, Lizzie dear, you really ought to tell! I'm sure that if you do, we can make you feel better."

"But I don't know whether I have good reason. If I told you what the matter was, you'd think I was a fool."

"Tell us and let us decide for ourselves," Clara said. "I promise I shan't think any such thing."

Lizzie took a deep breath. "I write to Mama every day, as you know, and she has always written back at once. But for the last few days, there's been no word and I can't help thinking something must be very wrong. Perhaps Mama has been taken ill. Or perhaps there's been an accident…the baby…"

Talking about her deepest fears, putting them into words for the first time, made Lizzie feel even worse. Tears were standing in her eyes when she finished speaking, and she blinked them away.

"I'm sorry…I don't know why I'm crying exactly. Only I can't bear to think of what may be happening at home."

"I think that's quite understandable," said Clara. "Come with me now and we'll see what Mama and Papa say about it."

"Oh, no! I couldn't bother them with my concerns. They've been so kind to me already," said Lizzie.

"Nonsense," said Clara. "They undertook to look after you while your mother is indisposed. Papa would be mortified if you did not confide in him. Come with me, Lizzie. I'm sure there's something that can be done to reassure you."

Chapter Seven

In which Uncle William speaks his mind

Aunt Victoria, Uncle Percy and Grandmama had finished their dinner and were sitting in the lamplight when Clara and Lizzie came into the drawing room. Hugh and Lucy remained outside the open door. They were, Lizzie knew, going to listen as best they could from there, for if all four children had burst into the room, they would certainly have been sent up to get ready for bed. Even Clara and Lizzie on their own were met with raised eyebrows from Aunt Victoria. The children were not permitted to come downstairs after dinner, except on very special occasions. Uncle Percy made a harrumphing noise, as though clearing his throat, and said, "Well now, to what do we owe the pleasure of this visitation? Lizzie, my dear, I should have thought it was nearly time for you to be thinking of getting ready for bed."

"Papa, Lizzie has something she wants to say to you. To ask you." Clara took Lizzie by the hand and led her to a spot on the carpet directly in front of Uncle Percy's chair. To Lizzie she said, "Go on. Tell Papa what you told me."

Lizzie wondered what everyone would say if she turned and ran from the room. Grandmama in particular was looking at her from behind the spectacles that she wore for reading with a rather disapproving expression. She was a great believer in proper bedtimes and she was frowning quite severely.

If Uncle Percy hadn't taken Lizzie by the hand and said, "Come, come child. No one here is going to be angry with you, you know. Tell us what's worrying you, do," she would have made her escape at once.

Instead, she took a deep breath. "I have not had a letter from Mama for several days, and it's not like her at all," she whispered. "I fear that something may have happened to her. Or perhaps to the baby, and she doesn't know how to tell me in a way which won't worry me."

"Cecily has always been a very conscientious letter-writer, it's true," said Grandmama to Lizzie, "but it is also true that someone during the late stages of your mother's condition may be indisposed and therefore unable to write."

"I'm sure that Mama would put a few words on paper however ill she was," said Lizzie. "That is exactly why I...why I'm worried about her."

"I'm sure there's no reason to be frightened," said Uncle Percy. "I shall write to her myself and inquire.

In a few days, we will know more, I feel certain. Go to bed now, my dear, and don't let it trouble you any longer."

Lizzie stood staring at Uncle Percy's feet, not knowing what to do. Only now, when she saw that there was to be *still* more waiting, did she realize how much she'd been hoping for immediate comfort. She felt so disappointed that her eyes filled with tears and she turned away to hide them.

Uncle William, who had been sitting silently up to that moment, suddenly stood up and strode over to Lizzie. She flinched a little and then immediately felt sorry, and wished she could have smiled welcomingly at her uncle instead. It wasn't Uncle William's fault that he looked so frightening, but it was difficult not to be somewhat scared of him. She had never, it was true, seen him lose his temper, but Lucy had told her stories of smashed dishes and curtains pulled from the window.

Uncle William wasn't interested in her, however.

He came right up to Uncle Percy's chair and began to shout.

"You have no scrap of imagination, Percy. Can't you see the child is at her wits' end? What's the use of writing yet more letters and waiting and waiting? Don't you understand how endless the hours will be for Lizzie? Clearly, you don't. I refuse to stand here and let her go on and on being unhappy. I shall take the carriage as soon as possible…tomorrow morning…and drive Lizzie down to the country to visit her mama. I hope you all agree."

He glared round at the others. Grandmama looked as though she were about to say something, and Uncle William noticed this.

"Well, Mama? Do you wish to object?"

"No, no, my dear. I would only suggest that you wait until next Sunday, perhaps. After all, there is school to consider, is there not? We wouldn't wish Lizzie to miss her lessons, I'm sure."

"I don't care a fig for school and lessons and I have

no intention of letting this child wait for nearly a week. She'll be worn out by the end of that time. No, tomorrow it is. Percy, I may take the carriage, I presume?"

"I suppose you may, William," Uncle Percy said. "Are you sure you feel well enough for such a journey?"

"Well enough?" Now Uncle William was shouting again, even more loudly, and waving his arms in the air in a very alarming manner. "There's nothing wrong with me, except for the fact that I have lost an eye. I'm as strong as I ever was and I'll knock to the ground anyone who says different, that I will!"

"No one's suggesting that there's anything wrong with your health, my dear," said Grandmama, who seemed to be the only person in the family who could speak to William in a normal tone of voice. "I think Percy wonders whether you'll be able to remain calm enough when you arrive at Cecily's and make sure that you do not make any situation you find there even more…difficult."

Uncle William was suddenly silent. He looked crestfallen, and for a moment, Lizzie thought he might begin to weep from his one eye. He did not shed any tears, however, but instead sighed deeply and said, much more quietly, "I shall be as gentle as a lamb, never fear, Mama. I'm sure I shouldn't like to frighten poor Cecily. Nor you, Lizzie," he added, addressing Lizzie directly for the very first time since her arrival in London.

"No, sir," said Lizzie, trying to compose herself and hide her fears. "I'm sure I won't be frightened at all. And it's very kind of you to take me to visit Mama. I will be ready in the morning. Thank you."

She bobbed a curtsey at everyone and fled from the room. Hugh and Lucy stood back to let her pass, and the three younger children ran upstairs together. When they arrived breathless on the landing outside their bedrooms, Elsie the maid was just coming downstairs from the attic to set the table for the next day's breakfast.

"You're very late to bed, children," she said, smiling at them. "It'll be hard for you to rise and shine tomorrow."

"I'll be up at dawn, Elsie," said Lizzie. "I'm going to visit my mama in the country." She did not tell Elsie how nervous she felt at the prospect of being alone with Uncle William for the whole journey.

"I wish Uncle William would take me too," said Lucy. "I'd like to see the country. I've been to the seaside."

"I'm sure Uncle William has enough to worry about without having to deal with you too," Hugh said. "It's not going to be an outing, you know."

"I'm going to bed. You are the rudest brother that ever was!" said Lucy, flouncing into the bedroom. Lizzie followed her.

"Good night, Lizzie," said Hugh. "Wasn't it fun in the greenhouse today?"

"Yes," said Lizzie. "It was. I'd almost forgotten about it, what with all that's happened since we returned home. Good night."

෬

Lizzie lay in bed, wide awake and listening to Lucy, who was snuffling a little through her nose as she slept. What she had said to Hugh was quite true. She *had* almost forgotten about Mr. Hocking and the wonderful plants he was in charge of. Hugh had pointed out to her the banks of rhododendrons, which came from the highest mountains in the world, named the Himalayas. Captain Hardwicke had first brought them to England in 1799, and more recently, Sir Joseph Hooker had added many other varieties from India. Hugh had also told her about the tulips they would see in the spring and how once, long ago, the bulbs were worth as much as jewels. How pleasant it would be to work in a greenhouse like a palace and care for growing things! Or even dig in the earth in the flowerbeds outdoors. How wonderful it would be to be a lady gardener! Thinking about this distracted Lizzie from what was really keeping her awake: a dread of the long journey to Mama's cottage (and back!) with only Uncle William for company. What on earth would they find to say to one another? She hadn't been telling Uncle William the truth. She found that she was more than a little frightened having no one but him to speak to for hours and hours together.

Chapter Eight

In which Uncle William converses with Lizzie

"Are you comfortable, Lizzie?" said Uncle William, and Lizzie nodded. She was perched beside him on the high seat of the family carriage, because the day was fine, and she would have felt awkward sitting behind him as a passenger all by herself. Besides, she liked to look at the glossy chestnut backs of the horses. She wished that these beautiful creatures might live at the house, like Mrs. Tibbs, the cat, but she supposed that having horses grazing in the back garden would scandalize the neighbors. London was different from the country. There, everyone had fields near their houses where their horses could enjoy the open air, and the animals slept in stables nearby. But of course there was no room in London for every house to have a stable attached to it.

"Looking at the horses, are you?" said Uncle William, as he flicked the reins and they moved off. "Are you certain you are sitting comfortably, Lizzie? It can take time to get used to the motion. Fine creatures, horses. Understand every word you say to them. That's what I found, out in the Crimea."

Lizzie thought for a moment and then ventured a question. "Were you in the Cavalry?" She didn't know much about the Army, but she did know that the Cavalry rode horses and the Infantry had to march.

"No, not me. I had to walk across the battlefield. It made no difference, mark you. Bullets and swords find you wherever you are. But I did feel sorry for the poor horses, all the same. They never thought, did they, that they'd end up in a battle. They didn't know what was happening. Pitiful. It was enough to break your heart, seeing the unfortunate creatures with blood all over them, dead in the dirt."

Uncle William turned to Lizzie and added, "D'you know the poem by Lord Tennyson?

Stormed at with shot and shell,

Boldly they rode and well,

Into the jaws of Death,

Into the mouth of Hell

Rode the six hundred."

"*The Charge of the Light Brigade*…yes, we had to learn it at school."

"Lot of rot," said Uncle William. "Well, some of it is. Not the jaws of Death part. That's true enough. And the mouth of Hell, well, I hope I never have to see the real Hell, because if it's anything like the Crimea, then even the worst of sinners doesn't deserve such a fate."

"It must have been terrible," said Lizzie, partly hoping Uncle William would change the subject and partly fascinated to hear more. She had never met a real soldier before and she couldn't deny that however terrifying it was to think of dead men and horses covered in blood, however chilling it was to imagine the bullets whistling past your head and the swords slicing down all around you, there was also something exciting about the fact that the events Uncle William had witnessed were now part of History and there were even poems written about it, by famous poets like Lord Tennyson.

"Trouble with war is," Uncle William went on, "that people need to have heroes to worship. They need to hear stories about bravery and daring and victory. The other army needs to be thoroughly defeated and then everyone's happy. But I tell you, the real killer in the Crimea was disease. Disease and dirt. Cholera and dysentery killed more poor fellows than died in battle, I shouldn't wonder. But no one wants to read about sickness and dirt in their morning paper. No, they want glory!"

Uncle William sounded furious as he spoke. Lizzie wondered whether she dared to ask him about his missing eye. She plucked up her courage. "Uncle William, how did you lose your eye? It must have been so painful! I can't even think about it without tears springing to my eyes."

"Painful?" Uncle William fell silent for a moment. "I don't think anyone has ever asked me about that. Oh, don't mistake me. They're full of care and fussing around, but no one has asked me about the pain before. When my mother first saw me, when I came home from the war, she burst into tears, and Victoria fainted dead away. Dead away. Even Percy was silenced by the sight of me. I had a bandage around my head then, of course, and I was as thin as a skeleton after not eating properly for months. But I was alive. That was the thing that I clung to, through the pain. I was alive. So many others were lying dead in that wilderness. But the pain. I don't know how to describe it. As though fire and rocks and biting creatures have taken up residence in your head. A tearing and a throbbing and a burning. Impossible to tell anyone what it's like, in truth. I don't have the words. Lord Tennyson would find it hard to describe, I'd warrant."

"How did it happen?" Lizzie wanted to know everything, now that Uncle William had started telling her about it.

"A bayonet wound. I suppose I can't complain, for the man I was attacking came off worse. I killed the poor fellow." Uncle William grunted.

Lizzie couldn't help it. She covered her face with her hands and shivered.

"Next thing I know," Uncle William continued, "I'm on a stretcher and being taken off to the hospital. And that I *am* glad of. She cared for me, you know. The Lady with the Lamp. Florence Nightingale herself. I'd be dead if it weren't for her. Everyone thinks of her as a gentle soul, an angel. Well, she was angelic and no mistake, but as tough as the most battle-hardened general as well. No one dared to disobey her. Woe betide you if she found dirt where it shouldn't have been. Cleanliness, that was the secret. Keeping everything clean, she insisted on that. She wiped my forehead. With her own hands. I had a fever, you see. For days and days I didn't know where I was, or who I was and she didn't give up. She wiped my brow and dressed my eye and held my hand and all the while I was having such dreams. You would not believe the strangeness of fever dreams. I saw monsters. Horses with tails made of fire. Fish with a woman's eyes. Men with their heads growing at the ends of their hands... Oh, I shouldn't be telling you this. It's not fit for a young girl to hear."

"No, it's as good as any story, Uncle William. Really. No one's ever told me anything like this before." A thought occurred to her. "Do you still have bad dreams?" she said. She felt shaken by what she'd been told, but didn't want to speak of her feelings.

"Often," said Uncle William. "Sometimes the dreams are so bad I'm frightened of going to sleep. So I stay awake too long and then I'm tired and cross during the day. Your cousins think I'm a very bad-tempered sort, and that's true, I suppose, but it's only because of the pain. I still have pains in my head. Miss Nightingale couldn't do anything for those, alas, though I don't get them as often as I used to. I must hope that I will mend entirely one of these days."

"Oh, I hope so most sincerely, Uncle William," said Lizzie.

Uncle William smiled at her. It was as though the sun had come out from behind the darkest of clouds. She realized that she had never seen her uncle smile before, not once. The sight warmed her.

"Your father's death…that was a blow to me, Lizzie," Uncle William continued. "Percy is a good man, but John was my favorite brother. And your mama…well, I always thought of her as a jewel among women. When you said you were worried about her, why, I found it impossible not to be worried myself. I would hate any harm to come to Cecily."

They had left London far behind them now, and both of them fell silent. Lizzie hadn't noticed the time going by, but she saw that they must have traveled quite a long way. The trees, some of them with all their leaves gone, were bending in the strong wind. Heavy, gray clouds covered the sky and the chill in the air meant that winter was truly upon them. Uncle William had tucked a rug around Lizzie's legs before they set off, but still she felt stiff and cold. She began to worry about Mama. What if she was lying ill in bed and didn't recognize her daughter? What then? Perhaps, though, all would be well. She thought longingly of firesides and the warmth that awaited them in the cottage.

As they drove at last into the village, Lizzie's spirits rose. Now that they were passing the Huntsman's Inn, now that they were coming up the lane to the cottage, her heart began to beat faster and faster. She was longing to see Mama and hold her and kiss her…

"Are you feeling brave, young Lizzie?" Uncle William asked. "I'm sure all will be well, but we'll be prepared, will we not? *Into the mouth of Hell*, like the six hundred, don't you know! Ready for anything."

Lizzie nodded, unable to speak. She had noticed that no smoke rose from the chimney of the cottage. Surely no one would neglect to light a fire in this weather. The carriage drew to a halt and Uncle William helped her to climb down. She didn't feel as if she were ready for anything. She stood beside her uncle as he lifted the brass knocker and let it drop onto the wooden front door. There was no answer, so Uncle William knocked again. Lizzie was just about to suggest that they go around to the back of the house when the door opened and there was Eli Bright, dressed, as always, in black from head to toe. He regarded Lizzie without smiling and then lifted his gaze to Uncle William.

"Good day to you, sir," Uncle William said. "I am William Frazer and I've brought my niece to visit her mother."

"I suppose you must come in, then," said Eli Bright, without so much as a single word of welcome or greeting. "I shall tell her you're here to see her."

He stepped into the dark interior of the cottage and Lizzie and Uncle William followed him. Lizzie was trembling. What would they find?

Chapter Nine

In which Lizzie and her mother are reunited

The interior of the cottage was so dark that Lizzie found it hard to make out the familiar furnishings and features of her old home. But there they were: the shabby armchairs next to the empty grate. Why had no fire been lit to take the chill off the room? The table still stood beside the window. It was covered by the plush cloth that Lizzie knew was almost as old as she was. The mantelpiece over the fire had nothing more decorative on it than a clock.

"To what do we owe this unexpected visit?" Mr. Bright inquired, looking as though the visit was far from a pleasure.

"Young Lizzie here was worried about her mama. She has not written for some time, and knowing that she is in a delicate condition, we were concerned for her welfare." Uncle William looked around the dark, chilly room and stared at Mr. Bright out of his one good eye. Lizzie, meanwhile, was edging toward the stairs. She could no longer keep silent. Her eagerness to be reunited with her mama was almost overwhelming.

"Is Mama upstairs?" she asked. "May I go up? And where is Annie?"

"I have dismissed Annie. Her wages were a drain upon the household. And besides, she was growing quite old and infirm. It was a kindness to her."

"But," Lizzie was almost speechless with distress.

"Why did Mama not tell me? How could you send Annie away before I could say goodbye? And how can Mama manage all on her own? I want to see her. Is she in her bedroom? I must see her!"

"Your mother is resting. She is asleep, I've no doubt. Perhaps you would wait while I go and see."

"Nonsense, man!" Uncle William burst out. "Can't you see that Cecily would much rather be woken by her daughter than by anyone else in the world? How can you be so cruel as to make her wait after such a long journey? And you can see how distressed she is. Go on, Lizzie. He's not going to stop you."

Lizzie could see that Mr. Bright was taken aback by being spoken to in this manner. He took a step backward and let his mouth fall open in amazement. She decided to leave him to Uncle William, who would doubtless know how to deal with him. She tiptoed upstairs as quickly as she could, and knocked on her mother's bedroom door. There was no answer.

Lizzie stood outside on the little landing in some

confusion. She hesitated to wake her mama, if indeed she was asleep, because everyone knew that when you were expecting a baby, you grew very tired and needed rest above all things. But Mama would certainly want to see her. Surely she's missing me, Lizzie thought, as much as I'm missing her? She decided to knock once more and go in.

The sight that met her eyes when she opened the door nearly made her cry. Her mother was indeed asleep, but her room was so bare and unwelcoming; the linen on the bed so sparse and shabby; the curtains at the windows so grubby and thin that as far as Lizzie could see, anyone who slept here would close her eyes the second she got into bed to avoid looking around. Was it, she wondered, that the room was always like this and she was only noticing it for the first time because she had grown used to the comfort and luxury of the house in Chelsea? Or had matters changed since her departure? She had only been gone a few weeks. Could such alterations happen in so short a time?

And her mama! Cecily's light-brown curls were in disarray and looked as though they hadn't been brushed for a long time. Her mother's face was pale, too, and her lips, in the dim light of the room, had lost all color. If Lizzie hadn't known she was expecting a baby, she would have thought she was looking down at an invalid.

"Mama?" she whispered, touching her mother's shoulder gently. "Mama, wake up. It's me. It's Lizzie, come to see you."

Her mother stirred and opened her eyes. For a moment, she was silent, staring at her daughter, then she struggled to sit up.

"Lizzie! Lizzie, my dear! You're real! Oh, you're here. You're really here, my precious child. I thought you must be just another fragment of my dream. I dream about you so often…are you real?"

"Yes, of course I'm real, Mama." Lizzie flung herself onto the bed, and put her arms around her mother's neck and kissed her. The familiar smell, the smell of her mother's skin that she had known since childhood, was there, but overlaid with a kind of sourness, as though her mother had been perspiring under the bedclothes, or as though…could it be true? …she hadn't bathed lately.

As if she had been reading Lizzie's thoughts, Cecily said, "Oh, I must smell dreadful. It's such a business, heating up the water for a bath. And I am too weak to make the effort."

"But why?" Lizzie asked. "Why are you in bed the whole day? Is it because Annie is no longer here to take care of you? Oh, Mr. Bright is very wicked to send her away! Are you ill? If you are, we must call the doctor."

"No, no, not ill at all. Just the normal aches and pains of someone in my condition. And I stay in bed to save heating the parlor. We do not have a great deal of money. Dismissing Annie has saved us a little. But don't let's talk about that now. It's so wonderful to see you. How is it that you're here? Is something wrong in London?"

"Uncle William brought me in the carriage. I was worried about you. You haven't written for such a long time."

"I'm so sorry, my darling," said Cecily. "Eli persuaded me that too much letter-writing would tire me out, and only permits me to write to you once a week."

"That is the most dreadful thing I ever heard!" said Lizzie. "How does he dare to tell you when you can and can't write?" She did not dare to say so, but she thought that Mama might at least have written to tell her about Mr. Bright's decision, in order to stop her from worrying. She thought that this was easily the most wicked thing he'd ever done.

Tears stood in her mother's eyes, and Lizzie was instantly sorry.

"I'm so sorry for shouting at you, Mama. I didn't mean it, really. And perhaps you are too weak to write to me. It doesn't matter about the letters. I will do without them if only I know you are well."

"You're a kinder daughter than I deserve, Lizzie. And I will write in the future, I promise. I will tell Eli that I will, yes. But now I must get up and greet your uncle."

Cecily pushed back the bedclothes and struggled out of bed. She said to Lizzie, "Go downstairs and wait for me there. I will dress and come down. You and Uncle William must take some refreshment with us. I'm sure we have enough to share, however humble it may be."

"I don't think you ought to cook, Mama. You don't look strong enough."

"You go down, dear. Tell Eli and Uncle William that I'll be there as soon as I can."

"I'd rather stay and help you to dress, Mama. Will you allow me to do that? I could arrange your hair."

"No, my dear, I'll be quicker on my own. You go downstairs, there's a good girl."

Lizzie went down to the parlor feeling quite powerless. Her heart was heavy when she considered how little she could do to help her mother.

Chapter Ten

In which Uncle William takes action

Lizzie did as she was told. Down in the parlor, Uncle William was standing at the window, staring out at the small back garden, and Mr. Bright was seated at the table. Had they spoken at all while she was upstairs? It was hard to tell. She turned to Mr. Bright.

"Mama will be down in a moment. She says we're to take some refreshment with you."

"Indeed?" He didn't go on and Lizzie wondered whether "indeed" meant that he was pleased or displeased at the idea of company for lunch. That was the thing that had most angered her about Mr. Bright. You never knew what he thought. His words were all of a piece: dull and flat and the very opposite of lively, whatever he wanted to say. She was wondering whether she had the courage to ask directly, when she heard her mother coming downstairs and stepping into the room.

"Cecily!" said Uncle William and he caught her up in a bear hug, lifting her off the floor and whirling her around as though she were nothing more than a child.

"William! How wonderful to see you! And in such good spirits, too. How are you?"

"Please," said Mr. Bright, frowning. "My wife is in a delicate condition. Your display of feeling is most unsuitable at such a time."

"Nonsense," said Uncle William. "Nothing I've done will harm either Cecily or her child." He turned back to Cecily. "I'm very well, I'm sure," he went on. He held Lizzie's mother at arm's length and looked very carefully at her. "Which is more than can be said for you, dear Cecily. You're pale, and you weigh not much more than Lizzie here, I'll be bound. Do you eat? Do you drink milk? Are you resting?"

"Yes, yes," said Cecily. "I'm doing very well."

"That's not what it looks like to me," said Uncle William. "What do you think, Lizzie?"

Lizzie was dismayed. Her mother's dress, when she compared it with the clothes that Aunt Victoria wore every day, was almost worn out. She remembered it from before she left the cottage, but at that time she hadn't realized that there were other dresses, other fabrics in the world which didn't have the weight and substance of a rag. Perhaps Mama was saving her good clothes until after the baby was born. She had arranged her hair and washed her face, but she was still just as pale and there were deep purple shadows under her eyes.

"You don't look like yourself, Mama," Lizzie said finally, not wanting to alarm her mother.

"Your daughter was concerned, Cecily," Uncle William added. "She wondered why you stopped writing to her."

"I've explained to Lizzie," said Cecily. "Mr. Bright has said that a letter once a week would be sufficient."

"Indeed, I did," said Mr. Bright. "Writing once a day is far too onerous for one in your condition. No one needs to write every day, I feel sure."

"That's not for you to decide," said Uncle William. "Although I can see that you have decided many things in this house."

"Cecily is my wife," said Mr. Bright. "I have a right to make decisions concerning her health and welfare."

"Health and welfare!" Uncle William was roaring by now. "How can even the most miserly of creatures find health and welfare in a hovel such as this? When my brother was alive, this was a place of comfort and ease and you have turned it into a kind of prison for Cecily.

In fact, I have seen prisons that are more luxuriously appointed than this."

Lizzie watched her mother as Uncle William spoke. She was sitting down now, on one of the two armchairs beside the grate and had covered her mouth with her hand. Mr. Bright was shocked into silence. Uncle William had just got into his stride, however. He marched into the tiny pantry, and called out over his shoulder, "Food! There is not enough food here to satisfy the mice! How dare you offer us refreshment when you know the state of your larder? Three eggs and the stale heel of a loaf of bread. Is this an adequate sufficiency for anyone? Anyone at all?"

"Today is market day," said Mr. Bright. "We will be going to buy our provisions later this afternoon. After your departure."

"Then you had best prepare yourself to go alone. Cecily, I am taking you to London with me. My brother's ghost would come and haunt my bedside if I left you here. Please go upstairs with Lizzie now and put a few necessities into a suitcase. We will be leaving shortly. We will lunch at the Huntsman's Inn."

"But…" Mr. Bright's composure was deserting him. He was opening his mouth to object when Uncle William growled, "I will strike you, sir, if you prevent me. If you wish to see your wife and child restored to you at any time in the future, I advise you to permit this short… holiday, let us call it…and raise no further objections."

"On the contrary," said Mr. Bright. "I feel Cecily will greatly enjoy a short stay with her relations in London. Her absence will allow me to save enough funds, perhaps, to make her life easier when she returns. We are, you see, very short of funds."

"Hmm," said Uncle William. "It may be that you are, but I cannot believe that you do not make enough money to keep you clothed and fed, at least. There's a great difference between abject poverty and purposely living as cheaply as one can. I know that my brother left enough money to provide for his wife and child. Have you spent all that?"

"Certainly not. My wife's inheritance is safely in the bank. I was brought up to believe that one did not squander one's capital. There is such a thing as saving money."

"There is also such a thing as being a miser and a skinflint!" said Uncle William. "Go, Cecily. Go and pack your suitcase. You are coming with me and Lizzie."

☙

The carriage was approaching London as dusk fell. The violet sky was studded with bright stars on this frosty night and, all over the city, lamps were lit and shining behind drawn curtains. Lizzie, who had fallen asleep for a little while after their good lunch of beef and roast potatoes at the Huntsman's Inn, woke up and looked at her mother. Already, even after such a short while away from Mr. Bright, Cecily was looking happier, although she was still pale, and getting ready for the journey had tired her greatly. Lizzie felt content. All would be well, now that her mother was in London with her. They could forget about the chilly, comfortless cottage and the chilly, comfortless person who remained there by himself.

As the carriage drew up in front of the house, Lizzie said to Uncle William, "What will Uncle Percy say when he sees Mama?"

"Yes, William," said Mama. "It won't perhaps be convenient to have yet another person thrust upon the household."

"Look at this house, Cecily! Look at the size of it! Why, you could fit your cottage into it three times over and have room to spare. Percy and Victoria will be delighted. As for my mother, well, she likes nothing better than visitors and is forever complaining that we do not see enough company. Come, we will surprise them all."

He helped Cecily out of the carriage and Lizzie followed them up the steps. Now that they were at the house, she wondered whether indeed everyone would be as delighted as Uncle William said they'd be at the prospect of another mouth to feed and another body to accommodate.

Chapter Eleven

In which Lizzie's mama receives a letter

Lizzie was right. She couldn't say so to anyone, but she could see that when Uncle William turned up with Mama in the carriage, the family was somewhat surprised. Of course, they were all most welcoming and the house was certainly big enough to accommodate Cecily, but still, Lizzie knew that her arrival would mean something of an upheaval and, of course, there would soon be a baby and a nursery maid would have to be hired.

Uncle William told such hair-raising stories of the cottage and the behavior of Mr. Bright that everyone agreed he couldn't possibly have left his sister-in-law in such a situation. Uncle Percy simply said, "Well, all's well that ends well. That is all. Cecily is in grave need of support and shelter and we are happy to provide it. You're welcome, my dear."

On her first night in London, Lizzie's mother slept on a day-bed in the morning room, but the very next day the whole house was turned upside down, it seemed, as Aunt Victoria and Grandmama decided who was to give up their room for the new arrival. In the end, after much discussion, it was arranged. Cecily would have Lucy and Lizzie's room and the two girls would move in with Clara.

"I hope you're not too upset, Clara," said Lizzie, as she arranged her clothes in the new chest of drawers.

"I leave the grumbling to my little sister," said Clara.

"She's the one who seems most put out. I am sorry not to have my own room any longer, but it can't be helped. Hugh couldn't move in with you, and I don't think Uncle William would be comfortable in the attic, as he suggested. No, this is the best arrangement. After all, your mother will soon have a baby to care for, so she will need a larger bedroom than Hugh's in any case."

"It won't be for long," said Lizzie. "Mama intends to rest here for a few weeks and then return to the cottage."

As she spoke, she began to dread that day, but how was it to be prevented? How could she keep her mother here in London when Mama's husband was elsewhere and where, besides, she was creating so much inconvenience, whatever everyone said to the contrary?

Clara said, "She is welcome for as long as she wishes to stay, you know. For my part, I would love to care for a small baby. I am going to enroll at the nursing school next year, whatever Mama and Grandmama say. I've been persuading Papa of my unwavering desire to be a nurse whenever I happen to be alone with him and he's said that perhaps he would speak to them both. All nurses have to know about babies, do they not?"

"Yes, I'm sure they do," said Lizzie. "And you'd be such a good nurse, Clara."

CB

For a few days after her mother's arrival, Lizzie quite forgot about her walnut, but when she remembered, she went at once to see how it had grown. Her disappointment when she saw that nothing had happened nearly made her cry. She resolved to be much more attentive in the future. So, every day, Lizzie went out to the garden and gazed into the cold frame, looking at the pot in which she had buried her walnut. She was beginning to think that maybe she had dreamed it all. It was hard to believe in a growing thing if it showed no signs of growth. All she could see in the pot was brown earth and more brown earth, and each time she visited the cold frame, Lizzie made a fervent wish, in the hope of persuading her walnut to grow.

"Please, little walnut, come out. Come out soon. You've been asleep for a very long time and you must wake up now. Please come out. Oh, I do wish you would!"

She made quite sure that no one was listening when she whispered these words. Lucy would have thought she was very silly and she did not dare to guess what Hugh would have said. Lizzie herself knew that it was not a scientific way to make plants come out of the earth, but she didn't think it would do any harm.

❧

Shortly before Christmas, Uncle Percy received a letter from Mr. Bright. He summoned the whole family to the drawing room to hear what it said.

"I have here," he announced, "a letter from Cecily's husband, Mr. Eli Bright. I have already read it to Cecily and indeed she has received a letter too, with much the same information, though that is private to her, of course. I wish to tell you all what Mr. Bright says, because it will affect our life as a family and our future for the next few months at least." He coughed. "I shall read you the letter now: *Since my wife left me at the persuasion of your brother, I have been considering what is best for us all to do. I understand that life here is not as comfortable as it might be, but that is simply out of my desire to economize and my dislike of spending good money on frivolities. I believe that we all have too much luxury and that our reward for going without in this world will be riches in the next.*

Since Cecily is being cared for by you for the moment, I have taken the opportunity to put into action a plan I have nurtured for a long time. I am setting sail for West Africa in a few days' time, and intend to see whether the Church will be able to make use of me as a missionary there. Perhaps Cecily will join me in Africa when our child is old enough to travel safely to foreign parts. Until that time, I am grateful indeed that she has a family willing to care for her welfare and that of our child…"

Uncle Percy looked around. "The rest of the letter is not relevant."

Lizzie found that her heart was beating very fast. What did this mean? Surely Mama wouldn't think of going to live in Africa, even after the baby was old enough to travel. What would become of me, thought Lizzie, if she did? Uncle Percy was speaking again…

"I've considered this matter carefully and decided that we should do nothing for the moment. William will go down to the cottage and make inquiries about renting it out for the time being. When Cecily's child is born, and once the weather is warmer, we will see whether she can return to her home, with Lizzie and her new baby. But, until then, I am happy that we can give them a comfortable home. And, of course, it is out of the question for a very young child to travel to such an inhospitable climate. Mr. Eli Bright will have to resign himself to visiting England on home leave for the time being."

"Yes, indeed," said Grandmama. "I would not wish

a grandchild of mine to go traveling about the globe in his infancy. Home's best and for the moment, this is your home, Cecily. I would not wish John's widow to lack for anything."

Lizzie thought that Grandmama's words were fine and kind, but her grandmother didn't look as though she relished the thought of this extended stay. Lizzie, however, could hardly believe her good fortune. It seemed that she and Mama would be living in London for the present. How strange it would be to have Mr. Bright so far away, and what a relief it would be not to have to see him in the near future. Maybe they would stay long enough for her to plant her walnut in the garden. She determined to ask Mr. Lewin, or perhaps even Mr. Hocking, if they visited Kew Gardens in the spring, when would be the best time to transfer her plant from the flowerpot to its proper home in London soil.

Chapter Twelve

In which Lizzie has
a sleepless night

Christmas was Lizzie's favorite time of the year. Mr. Dickens's story named *A Christmas Carol* was, she thought, a very fine book indeed, with its ghosts and the best ending of any story she had ever read. As the holiday approached, she grew more and more excited. All over the house, everyone was making preparations. Cook and Elsie had a huge goose, plucked and drawn and ready to stuff, lying on the wooden table in the kitchen; there was a fat plum pudding already made and waiting to be heated for the Christmas dinner. Grandmama herself had supervised the roasting of a gigantic side of ham, making sure that it was well-studded with cloves and basted with a spicy mixture of cinnamon, nutmeg and honey.

Uncle Percy and Uncle William had brought in a young spruce tree and installed it in the drawing room in a bucket which would, in time, be covered up with a strip of wallpaper striped in red and gold.

"We'll be as grand as they are at Windsor Castle," said Uncle Percy, "with a tree that Prince Albert himself might well envy."

"May we help to decorate it, Papa?" asked Lucy. "Please say we may!"

"Only if you let Clara and Lizzie keep an eye on you to make sure that you don't eat all the gingerbread as you put it up. And the candles, of course, will be lit only when there are adults present. But yes, it will be a fine sight, I'm quite sure."

Lucy insisted on bringing Mrs. Tibbs the cat upstairs to see the ribbons and the pretty decorations Aunt Victoria had bought to make the tree beautiful, but Mrs. Tibbs was far more interested in the tempting smells wafting up from the kitchen and ran downstairs to where Cook and Elsie, in the indulgent spirit of the season, would allow her to eat the meaty scraps that had fallen onto the floor.

On Christmas morning, there were presents of fruit and nuts for all the children. Hugh and Lizzie each received a handsome wooden pencil case; Clara was given some pretty lace-edged handkerchiefs and Lucy a kaleidoscope.

Christmas dinner was a happy occasion. Lizzie was wearing her lovely new dress. The goose was roasted to perfection; the dessert was delicious and, by the end of the meal, everyone felt as though they never wished to eat another morsel ever again.

Cecily was sitting very upright in her chair and looking rather pale.

"Are you quite well, dear?" Grandmama asked, peering at Cecily through her spectacles.

"Yes, thank you. I believe I've eaten too much. A slight discomfort perhaps. It will soon pass. Indigestion, I suppose."

"Do you wish to withdraw?" Aunt Victoria asked.

"No, no," said Cecily and she tried to smile, but Lizzie thought that her mother didn't look quite herself.

"Let us raise our glasses," said Uncle Percy, just as Lizzie was wondering when they might leave the table. She wanted nothing more than to sit in the schoolroom and read quietly after all the rich food she had eaten. Hugh and Lucy were also looking full and red-faced and her mama, she could see, would have loved nothing better than to lie down in her bedroom. Still, Uncle Percy insisted on a toast. He raised his wineglass and said, "Health and happiness to us all. God bless us, every one!"

He winked at Lizzie, who recognized the quotation from *A Christmas Carol* and smiled back at her uncle. By the time the children were allowed to leave the table, night had fallen.

"Look!" said Hugh, when they were in the schoolroom. He had his nose pressed up against the window. "It's snowing."

"How lovely!" said Lucy. "Maybe tomorrow we'll be able to make a snowman in the garden."

ભ

Lizzie passed a very restless night. Perhaps, she thought, as she twisted and turned between sleep and wakefulness, I ate too much and my stomach is upset. I'm not used to such rich meat. Am I asleep? As she asked herself this question, she felt herself falling and falling and realized, even while she was dreaming, that she was, indeed, in a dream. There was banging and shouting somewhere far away and a voice saying, "Run! Be quick about it!" But no one she could see was running anywhere and the dream turned into one where she and Hugh were at Kew again, and the plants were growing all over the greenhouse like the roses around Sleeping Beauty's castle. Then the dream ended and Lizzie knew nothing further, till she heard Clara speaking quietly into her ear, and shaking her gently by the shoulder.

"Lizzie?" Clara said. "Lizzie, wake up. Can you hear something?"

Lizzie opened her eyes and saw that her cousin was standing beside her bed, with a shawl over her nightdress to protect her from the cold.

"Is it morning yet? It's still dark…" Lizzie said, drowsily.

"No, but listen. Can't you hear it?"

"I don't know what I'm listening for."

"I'm sure I heard a baby crying. I can't hear it now, but it woke me. Something woke me."

Clara gasped suddenly and added, "Your mama… it must be your mama. Perhaps she has given birth… But how is that possible? She was sitting at the dining table with us no more than a few hours ago. Surely we would have heard some comings and goings? Oh, but now I recall. Your mama thought she had indigestion during dinner. I suppose that must have been the beginning of her labor pains. Grandmama must have called the midwife, don't you think? Oh, Lizzie! We must go and have a look."

Lizzie got out of bed and put on her robe and slippers. She went to the door, which Clara had already opened. Sure enough, there were lights burning everywhere and Grandmama was standing outside Cecily's bedroom with her hair uncharacteristically in disarray. She had her sleeves rolled up and was wearing an apron over her robe.

"Grandmama, we heard a baby crying. Is it…?"

"Indeed it is!" said Grandmama. She came up to Lizzie and kissed her heartily. "You have a little brother, my dear. He gave no trouble being born; no trouble to speak of. Slipped out as though he couldn't wait to come into this world, even though we were not expecting him for a few weeks yet. We've washed him and your mother has fed him and she's resting now, but you may put your head around the door and peep at the little darling."

Clara burst out, "Oh, why didn't you call on me to help, Grandmama? I would have wanted to assist. You know how I love babies. And I've told you about my desire to be a nurse. This would have been a perfect opportunity for me to learn about childbirth."

"A baby being born is more than a lesson in nursing skills," said Grandmama, rather sharply. She went on a little more gently. "To tell the truth, dear, there wasn't time. Cecily went into labor shortly after you'd all gone to bed, and Uncle William ran down the road to fetch the midwife. I was in attendance; Cook and Elsie helped with the heating of the water. Everything was over before you could turn around. You will have plenty of opportunity to help from now on, you may be sure. Babies create a tremendous amount of work for everyone."

Lizzie opened the door of the room that had lately been hers and Lucy's. She, too, was angry at herself for sleeping through her brother's arrival in the world. All the noises and shouting she had thought she was hearing in her dreams must have been real. The curtains were still drawn and the bedroom was almost completely dark. In the light from the landing, Lizzie could make out a cradle, next to the bed.

"Mama?" she whispered. "Mama, are you awake?"

"Yes, Lizzie. Come and see."

Lizzie tiptoed to the bed and flung her arms around her mother's neck.

"Oh, Mama, Mama, are you well? I wish I'd woken up and then I'd have been here to help you."

Cecily laughed. "I needed very little help, I'm happy to say. You took your time being born but your brother was in a hurry to arrive."

"May I look at him, Mama?"

"Of course. He's sleeping soundly now."

Lizzie thought that she had never seen anything

half as beautiful as her baby brother. His little head was covered in soft, dark down and his tiny, tiny fingers were curled around the satin ribbon that bound the edge of his blanket.

"What's his name to be, Mama? What are we going to call him?"

"I have decided on John, after your papa, and William after your uncle. John William."

"Johnny," said Lizzie. "My brother Johnny. How I love him already!"

"I want you to do me a favor, Lizzie."

"Anything, Mama. I will do anything."

"Then please will you write to Eli? Tell him about the birth and that I am well and will write soon. Letters take a few weeks to reach him in Africa, but he must know as soon as possible. After all, Johnny is his son, too. Tell him about his child, and how beautiful he is."

"Of course I will, Mama," said Lizzie. She did not look forward to the task, but at least she would know what to say, and the letter did not have to be very long, after all. "I will write it this afternoon and show it to you before it's sent."

"Thank you, my dear. I can see how your eyes keep going back to the baby. He is handsome, is he not? I'm sure he will love you, his big sister, above everyone else."

Chapter Thirteen

In which the Frazer family learns to live with an infant

On the afternoon of Boxing Day, the day that Johnny was born, Lizzie and Hugh and Lucy had gone out into the garden and swept up all the snow they could find to make a small snowman. Lucy had wanted the snowman to be a snow baby, but that was judged too difficult a task by Hugh and Lizzie and the ensuing argument had driven all three children indoors after a while. They hadn't returned to their half-made creature, and when the thaw came, it melted into the grass and was gone.

Since that day, three weeks had passed and the weather was dull and rainy. Lizzie had almost decided that her walnut was dead. Surely it ought to have appeared by now? All over the garden, snowdrops were showing their bright flowers in the grass and yet her walnut refused to grow at all. She felt very disappointed.

"Who would have thought such a tiny scrap of a child could turn a whole household upside down in less than a month?" said Grandmama, gently rocking little Johnny on her knee. Lizzie watched the two of them and thought that the time had flown by more quickly than she could have imagined.

The baby was swaddled in a cloth and had just been fed by his mama. Now he was in the morning room, being admired by everyone. Lucy treated him as an honorary pet, though she often remarked that he was not as entertaining as Mrs. Tibbs. "He doesn't do anything," she said. "When he is fed, he goes to sleep and when he is hungry, he cries and cries and we all have to take turns to walk him along in his carriage or rock him in the cradle. I hope he will become more interesting as he grows older." She did not sound optimistic.

"Young animals," said Hugh, "are much better at getting on in the world. Young cats or dogs can walk about almost as soon as they're born and they don't seem to need half the care and attention that human babies do. I wonder why that is. And feeding and sleeping are such a problem. Have you ever heard of a kitten who can't sleep?"

"I'm glad to say that Johnny is a good sleeper for the most part. Much better than you were, Hugh." Grandmama smiled at her eldest grandson. "I can recall you at this age, you know. I can even recall your papa when he was newborn."

Lucy laughed. "How funny to think of Papa in a swaddling cloth! I cannot imagine it."

"Nevertheless, he was. And so were you, Miss Lucy. You were the most troublesome baby I ever knew and hardly allowed your poor mother a single undisturbed night."

Lizzie adored her little brother and looked forward to her turn to look after him. Mama had recovered well from the birth, and was now able to take her son out for walks and care for him, with help from the rest of the family.

Uncle Percy saw very little of the baby, because by the time he returned from the fabric shop, Johnny was generally asleep. Clara loved to wheel him down the road in his carriage, and sometimes, she would wake up for Johnny's night feed, roused by his cries. Then she enjoyed going into Cecily's bedroom to help her change the child's diaper and settle him down after he had drunk his fill.

"I wish I could look after him instead of going visiting all the time," Clara used to tell Lizzie. "You are lucky to be with him every day."

"Yes," said Lizzie, though privately she thought that Johnny perhaps demanded a little too much of everyone's energy. The baby was delightful, but no one seemed to have any time for anything except working to ensure his welfare.

The days and weeks passed quickly. Lizzie and Lucy and Hugh went to school every weekday. Lizzie had persuaded Hugh to tell her about some of his schoolwork, especially in mathematics, the sciences and geography, and she was learning many fascinating things: how plants germinated; how leaves became green; and how the clouds could show you what the weather was going to be like. It was finally a little warmer than it had been, but there were days when it was hard to believe that spring would ever arrive. It was still too chilly to hang the wash outside, and there seemed to be clotheshorses near every fire in the house on which various tiny garments had been draped to dry.

The walnut remained hidden in the earth in its

flowerpot. As far as Lizzie could see, there had been no progress at all. She mentioned this to Hugh one evening, when the two of them were working on some mathematical problems at the schoolroom table.

"You're not going to see anything, Lizzie. Not till it actually sprouts. There will be nothing but dark soil to look at till it puts out a shoot. All the growing and so forth is going on underground. If the earth were transparent, you would be able to see changes, I'm sure."

"Yes, I know I would." Lizzie sighed. "I'm sure it will sprout one day, but I'm just saying it's hard to believe in it, that's all."

"Forget about it, Lizzie. Help me with this problem."

Lizzie turned her attention to the problem in which three men were digging a ditch and taking their time over it, as far as she could see. All Hugh's problems in mathematics involved three men, and they were always engaged in the most boring activities you could imagine. She wished very much that there was something in the house that she might do that would make her feel useful and calm the restlessness she felt.

Chapter Fourteen

In which Clara comes into her own

By the middle of February, Lizzie had become quite used to having a little brother, but was growing more and more irritated both with her mother and with Lucy. Despite her earlier complaints about his inactivity, her youngest cousin had grown more and more fond of Johnny with every passing week, and Cecily indulged her, allowing her to carry the baby and cuddle him just as though she were his sister, and not merely his cousin. As soon as he opened his eyes – and sometimes even before that – Lucy was at his side, cooing and clucking and behaving in what Lizzie considered to be a really stupid manner.

Hugh turned out to be the only person Lizzie could confide in about this. She didn't want to bother her mother; Clara was often out visiting with Aunt Victoria and Grandmama and, when she returned home, she, too, was absorbed in the baby. Lizzie didn't mind her attentions as much as she did Lucy's because Clara was a more sensible person and Lizzie could see that her mama relied on her help a great deal.

"It's probably my fault," Lizzie said to Hugh one day when they were in the garden together, looking at the crocuses that had just begun to poke their mauve and yellow heads out of the soil. "If I did more, then Lucy wouldn't have the opportunity to interfere so much. But though I adore Johnny, I do find sitting beside a cradle and pushing it backward and forward a bit tiresome after a while. Is that a very dreadful thing? Please don't tell anyone what I'm telling you, Hugh. I'm a little ashamed not to be a better sister."

"You're a perfectly good sister," said Hugh. "And I wouldn't let Lucy bother you. When Johnny's old enough to choose, he'll be happier with you. You can teach him all sorts of things, like running and climbing and everything I've taught you, too, which will be much more exciting for him than Lucy's nonsense. She hasn't got a thought in her head that isn't about dolls or clothes or tea parties. He's not going to be interested in those."

They were near the cold frame and Hugh added, "Let's take a look at your walnut."

Lizzie shook her head as they peered through the glass. "Nothing at all. Sometimes I think nothing is ever going to happen, but then I remember Mr. Hocking saying that we had to be patient. That is what I am being, though I do long for a sign."

She didn't add that sometimes she wondered

whether Hugh had been right all along and whether her flowerpot might have been better indoors, but she wasn't going to admit this to him.

When they had left the cold frame, Lizzie pointed to a spot in one of the flowerbeds.

"That's where I shall plant it," she told Hugh. "When it has sprouted and grown a little. Then, when we're long dead, there will be a fine tree here."

"Let us hope it sprouts, then," said Hugh. "At this rate, we'll be long dead before even a single green shoot appears!"

೦ଽ

When Lizzie and Hugh returned to the house, they found everyone in a state of confusion. Uncle William was cradling little Johnny and rocking him back and forth in his arms. Aunt Victoria was comforting Lizzie's mama, who was weeping in an armchair, with her handkerchief pressed to her mouth. Grandmama was bustling about, telling Cook and Elsie what was needed for supper that evening, and when Hugh and

Lizzie came in, she turned to them with something like relief on her face.

"There you are, children. Now, there's not a moment to be lost."

Lizzie rushed to her mother's side. "What's the matter, Mama?" she cried. "What has happened?"

"Oh, Lizzie, it's poor little Johnny! He is not himself. No, not at all. He's not eating, and his face is flushed and hot and I think he might have a fever. Your grandmother is going to send for the doctor…oh, how I wish Johnny might be well again!"

"Let me go," said Hugh. "To fetch the doctor, I mean. I'll be there and back before you can blink."

"Yes, thank you, my dear," said Grandmama. "Run as fast as you can, and tell him to come at once."

Hugh had gone before anyone could say another word. Lizzie looked at him leaving the room and said, "I want to go. Please let me go. I can run just as fast as Hugh."

"I doubt that, my dear, but we won't argue about

it now," said Grandmama. "You may go to the shop instead and tell Percy and Clara, who went there only a short time ago, to come home at once."

Lizzie flung herself out of the front door and raced down the street in a fury. Grandmama has no idea how fast I can run, she thought. I shall show them. I shall show them all. She picked up her skirts and ran as fast as she could to the shop. As she went, she realized that Hugh had a far shorter journey to complete than she did. The doctor's house was in the next street and the shop was a good ten minutes' walk away. She didn't care. While she was running, it was hard to think of other things. All Lizzie's energies were concentrated on covering the ground as fast as she possibly could.

When she reached the shop, she almost fell into the door. Clara came around from behind the counter, and Uncle Percy found a stool for Lizzie to sit on, while her breathing returned to normal.

"It's Johnny," she gasped at last. "He's very sick, and Grandmama has sent me to fetch you both home."

C

For a little while, after the doctor had examined the baby and given him some medicine, matters became more peaceful. Little Johnny lay quietly in his cradle and Cecily, who was in the bed next to him, closed her eyes and fell asleep out of sheer exhaustion. The rest of the household hurried through the evening meal and then found they couldn't settle down to do anything. Even Lucy was subdued and went to bed much earlier than she usually did. By the time Lizzie came into the bedroom, she was fast asleep.

Lizzie lay in bed and closed her eyes. Please, she whispered – not quite sure whether she was praying to God or just wishing with all her heart – please let Johnny be well. I won't mind if Lucy cuddles him all day long. I won't care whether he loves me best or not. I'll take more care with my embroidery. I'll work harder at school. I'll be kind to everyone. Please let him be well.

Lizzie didn't remember falling asleep, but she must have, because suddenly she realized that there was someone in the bedroom, speaking to Clara. She struggled to sit up and saw, in the light from the landing, that it was her mother, leaning over Clara's bed.

"Mama!" she whispered. "What's the matter?"

"Nothing, dear. I'm just speaking to Clara."

"But why?"

"It's Johnny. He's hot again. I don't know what to do. I didn't want to rouse the whole household, but Clara said…"

"I told your mama that she must wake me if the baby took a turn for the worse. The doctor is coming again in the morning, but he has instructed me in exactly what needs to be done, and I'm going to do it. I know just what Johnny needs." Clara had risen from her bed and was dressing hurriedly.

"How do you know?" Lizzie asked, but she was too late. Her mother and her cousin had rushed from the room. Lizzie wondered what time it was, and just then she heard the grandfather clock in the hall chiming three.

The very middle of the night! She'd not often been awake at this hour and there was a special kind of silence all around as though the whole world were muffled and blanketed. She would have welcomed any sound at all, even Uncle William shouting out in his dreams, or her little brother loudly demanding his night feeding. What was happening in her mother's bedroom? What was Clara doing? What did she mean by knowing what had to be done? Lizzie knew that she was wide awake now and she knew she would not fall asleep again. Her curiosity was overwhelming. She got out of bed, and put on her robe and slippers.

The door to Mama's bedroom was open. Lizzie peeped around it and saw that Clara had taken Johnny out of his cradle and laid him on the bed. She had removed all his blankets and he was dressed in nothing more than a diaper and a cotton nightshirt. Mama was sitting next to the baby on the bed, and

holding him as Clara repeatedly took something…
a cloth? It was hard to see from where Lizzie was
standing…and dipped it into the basin full of water
that stood on the floor next to her feet. Then she
wrung it out and stroked it across the baby's forehead
and arms and legs, over and over again, not stopping
even for a moment.

Lizzie came up to her mother and said, "Oh, Mama!
How worried you look! Is Johnny…" She paused.
She couldn't say what she was thinking because it was
so dreadful that even uttering the words would have
made her cry. She wanted to know if her little brother
was going to die, but couldn't ask. What if the answer
was "yes"?

I won't be able to bear it if he dies, Lizzie thought.
He's so small, he's scarcely even lived. It's not fair to
let him die before he's had a chance to do anything…
to walk or talk or play or go to school. And what
will become of Mama if he's taken from her? Will I
be enough for her now that she's had a son? That

thought made Lizzie sadder than anything. "Can I do anything to help?" she said.

"No, thank you, Lizzie," said Clara, and Lizzie gazed at her cousin in astonishment. "All is well here. I am doing what needs to be done. Can you see? I am trying to make him cooler. He's too hot now. His fever is burning him up, poor little mite, but if we're patient and keep him cool with damp cloths, as I'm doing, then he'll soon be sleeping more peacefully. I've listened to Uncle William's stories of the Lady with the Lamp and how she used to do the same for the poor soldiers suffering from cholera and other terrible diseases. I am going to be a nurse, don't forget. This is what I shall be doing for much of the time, I expect. Fevers in childhood are very common."

Lizzie went to sit on the chair that her mother used to nurse the baby. No one needed her here, but she couldn't leave. She was too concerned about Johnny's health to go now, and she was soothed by Clara's quiet kindness and the way she betrayed not the slightest doubt that what she was doing was for the best. Why, she had even made Mama calm! That, surely, was a great gift to have if you wanted to become a nurse: the ability to give confidence to those who love the suffering person. At once, Lizzie relaxed. She would rest for a moment and then look at her brother again, to see if all was well. She closed her eyes and leaned against the back of the chair.

Chapter Fifteen

In which Lizzie has
two surprises

When Lizzie woke up, early morning light was coming through the bedroom curtains. Someone had covered her up with a blanket, but she felt chilly and stiff in all her limbs. She rose rather shakily to her feet and looked around her mother's bedroom. There was Mama, fast asleep on her pillows as though nothing worrisome had happened during the night. And there was the cradle with Johnny in it. Even from this distance Lizzie could hear the whiffling sound he made while he slept. She tiptoed over to look at her little brother and saw him lying on his stomach, with his face turned to the right and one of his arms flung up above his head. He looked...Lizzie hardly dared to hope, but she reached out to touch him and found his skin cool under her fingers. Tears began to flow unchecked down her cheeks. He wasn't going to die, after all. He would live and run about and speak and she would tell him the story of how Clara had saved his life. Lizzie knew that her cousin would deny that it was her doing. She would say, modestly, that Johnny would probably have recovered on his own with no help from her, but perhaps he would not have. Lizzie determined to tell everyone in the family exactly what she had seen Clara do, and she intended also to ask Mama to mention it to the doctor when he came for his visit. Now, surely, no one could prevent Clara from enrolling in Miss Nightingale's school, not when she had shown herself to be such an excellent nurse. Lizzie felt so happy that she wanted to shout and rouse the household, but she knew it was much too early for that.

Where could she go? What could she do till breakfast? Her joy was like something bubbling up within her. She felt so wide awake that she couldn't imagine ever wanting to sleep again. She knew that Elsie and Cook always rose very early to prepare breakfast, so she decided to go down to the kitchen and see if they might give her a cup of warm milk. Mrs. Tibbs was doubtless still in her basket, and it would be pleasant to play with her with no interference from Lucy.

"Why, Miss Lizzie," said Cook as she came into the warmth of the kitchen. "Whatever's up, dear? Can't you sleep?"

"I woke up very early," Lizzie answered. "So I thought I'd come and visit Mrs. Tibbs."

"She's gone out. It's a lovely day, and she likes to trot about when the dew's still on the grass. Likes to wet her little paws…that's what I think. There she is, behind the laurel bush."

"I'll go out and fetch her," said Lizzie and she made for the back door before Cook could realize how ill-dressed she was. Fortunately, there was so much to do in the kitchen, getting breakfast ready for the whole family, that the small matter of one of the children going outdoors in her nightgown and bedroom slippers was the furthest thing from Cook's mind.

Mrs. Tibbs was picking her way delicately through the damp grass.

"Come here, kitty!" said Lizzie, and she laughed. No, Mrs. Tibbs was quite determined. She settled herself near the cold frame and looked at Lizzie as if to say: *I'm not moving. This is a good sunny spot and here I shall stay.*

"Well," said Lizzie. "Since you seem set on remaining here, I shall have a look at my walnut. Though I don't suppose anything has changed since I last saw it."

She lifted up the glass, and peered down at her flowerpot. Then she looked more carefully and, still not quite believing the evidence of her own eyes, she picked up the flowerpot and examined it closely. And there it was: a tiny, green shoot, poking out of the dark earth all around it, and looking strong and vigorous to Lizzie, even though it was so small.

"You've sprouted!" she whispered to the little plant. "You're only a baby now, just like Johnny, but you'll both grow up strong and healthy. I know you will. Oh, what a wonderful morning this is!"

She put the flowerpot back in its place and closed the frame carefully. This was undoubtedly the best morning of her whole life. She knew that there was probably no connection (Hugh would say: *no scientific connection*) between the life bursting out of her walnut and the fact that her brother had been given another chance to thrive and flourish, but still she couldn't help linking them. She knew that as long as she lived, she would remember that the nut had put out its first greenness on the very day that Johnny recovered. Even when there was a sapling safely growing in the spot that she had chosen, she knew that she would be reminded of this day and of how happy she was. She felt as though every dream she had ever had might come true one day. She would have a lovely garden and work in it all by herself and bring thousands and thousands of plants into the world. And Johnny would help her. She would teach him exactly what he had to do.

Lizzie ran across the grass to the back door, not caring how wet her feet and the bottom of her nightdress had become, to wake the others and tell them her good news.

℘

Glossary

❦

serge – a hard-wearing heavy-weave fabric

pinafore – a sleeveless apron-like garment with ties or buttons at the back, worn over a dress

cold frame – a glass-topped box under which small plants are grown and protected from cold weather. The glass top lets the sunlight in so that the box acts like a miniature greenhouse

bombazine – a fabric made of silk and wool. Black bombazine was often worn by people in mourning

hoyden – a noisy/boisterous girl

woe betide – a phrase used to warn someone that they will be in trouble if they do something

Boxing Day – the day after Christmas Day. A public holiday in Britain

morning room – a sitting room, used during daylight hours. Less formal than a drawing room

Author's note

Almost the best thing about writing a book is being able to create a place for the characters to live in. The notion of having three books each set in the same place at different historical times was one that really appealed to me. Even more, it was the chance to work with two of the best children's writers around, who also happen to be friends. Writing is a lonely business and it was good to have someone who understood all the problems and could share the process of putting the story together. I've set my story just after the Crimean War, during the reign of Queen Victoria. I liked the idea of planting a seed in my book which Linda and Ann could develop in theirs.

I hope that everyone who reads my book will go on to see what happens in No. 6, Chelsea Walk as the years go by.

About the author

Adèle Geras was born in Jerusalem and before the age of eleven had lived in Cyprus, Nigeria and North Borneo. She studied languages at Oxford University and taught French before becoming a full-time author. She has written more than ninety books for children and young adults, including *Troy*, which was shortlisted for a prestigious UK children's book award, and its companion volume, *Ithaka*.

Adèle lives with her husband in Manchester, England.

To find out more about Adèle Geras, you can visit her website: www.adelegeras.com.

Usborne Quicklinks

For links to interesting websites where you can find out more about living in England in Victorian times, look around a Victorian house and play Victorian games, go to the Usborne Quicklinks website at www.usborne-quicklinks. com and enter the keyword "lizzie".

Internet safety

When using the Internet, make sure you follow these safety guidelines:

- Ask an adult's permission before using the Internet.
- Never give out personal information, such as your name, address or telephone number.
- If a website asks you to type in your name or email address, check with an adult first.
- If you receive an email from someone you don't know, don't reply to it.

Mary Ann & Miss Mozart
1764
ANN TURNBULL

Mary Ann's greatest wish is to become an opera singer, but when she is told she must leave her Boarding School for Young Ladies, her singing dreams are shattered. Distraught, she comes up with a plan to stay at school, oblivious to the danger it will put her in…

ISBN 9780794523329

Lizzie's Wish
1857
ADÈLE GERAS

When Lizzie's stepfather sends her to stay with relatives in London, Lizzie struggles to adapt to her new life of stiff manners and formal pastimes. She lives for the daily letters from her mother, but when the letters suddenly stop, Lizzie sets out to discover the truth and finds herself on a rescue mission.

ISBN 9780794523374

Cecily's Portrait
1895
ADÈLE GERAS

Cecily is enchanted when she meets Rosalind, a photographer, who seems to be the perfect match for Cecily's lonely widowed father. But her father's friend, the dull and dowdy Miss Braithwaite, keeps spoiling her plans to unite the pair. Will Cecily's dreams ever come true?

ISBN 9780794523343

Polly's March
1914
LINDA NEWBERY

When Polly discovers her new neighbors are suffragettes, fighting for women's right to vote, she is determined to join their protest march. But her parents are scandalized. Will she dare to defy them and do what she thinks is right?

ISBN 9780794523367

ও৪

Josie Under Fire
1941
ANN TURNBULL

When Josie goes to stay with her cousin, Edith, she tries to fit in by joining Edith and her friends in teasing a timid classmate. But when the bullying gets out of hand, Josie faces a dilemma: she knows what it feels like to be picked on, but if she takes a stand, will Edith tell everyone her secret?

ISBN 9780794523350

ও৪

Andie's Moon
1969
LINDA NEWBERY

Andie dreams of becoming an artist and loves living in Chelsea, with the fashion, music and art galleries along the trendy King's Road. There's even a real artist living in the apartment downstairs. Could Andie's paintings, inspired by the excitement of the first-ever moon landing, be good enough to win his approval?

ISBN 9780794523336